JOANNE ROCK

ONE COLORADO NIGHT

HARLEQUIN
DESIRE

HARLEQUIN®
DESIRE™

Recycling programs
for this product may
not exist in your area.

ISBN-13: 978-1-335-73571-3

One Colorado Night

Harlequin Enterprises ULC
22 Adelaide St. West, 41st Floor
Toronto, Ontario M5H 4E3, Canada
www.Harlequin.com

Printed in U.S.A.

Ryder's chest blocked the breeze from her back.

The cedar and leather scent of him stole around her. "You can't sacrifice personal happiness for someone who checks a bunch of boxes," he said. "It's a bloodless way to approach a relationship."

"Bloodless?" She spun around to face him. "You think I don't feel? That I make decisions like some kind of automaton?"

She felt the warmth of his breath on her face, the force of his frustration with her. Those gunmetal eyes sparked with an internal fire, the silver streaks near his pupils turning molten.

"Don't you?"

"How dare you. I feel. I have the same hungers coursing through my veins as you."

The force of them made her feel lightheaded. Dizzy with awareness of this man and all the things they'd once felt for each other.

She told herself to walk away.

But at the same moment, Ryder's mouth descended toward hers.

* * *

One Colorado Night by Joanne Rock
is part of the Return to Catamount series.

Dear Reader,

I'm excited to return to Catamount, Colorado, where this month Jessamyn Barclay is having a turn at wrestling with the Barclay family drama.

For all her seeming success on the outside, Jessamyn is poised to crash and burn when she's reunited with long-ago crush Ryder Wakefield. It hardly seems fair when she's trying to impress the One Who Got Away. But if there's one thing I've learned from life and romance novels, it's that happily-ever-afters have to be fought for. And Jessamyn is in for a major battle as she goes head-to-head with Ryder, especially once she learns the secret he's been keeping from her!

I hope you're enjoying the Return to Catamount series. Next month, Lark Barclay comes to town, and you won't want to miss the sparks that fly when she runs into her hockey star ex-husband.

Happy reading,

Joanne Rock

Joanne Rock credits her decision to write romance after a book she picked up during a flight delay engrossed her so thoroughly that she didn't mind at all when her flight was delayed two more times. Giving her readers the chance to escape into another world has motivated her to write over eighty books for a variety of Harlequin series.

Books by Joanne Rock

Harlequin Desire

Dynasties: Mesa Falls

The Rebel
The Rival
Rule Breaker
Heartbreaker
The Rancher
The Heir

Return to Catamount

Rocky Mountain Rivals
One Colorado Night

Visit her Author Profile page at Harlequin.com, or joannerock.com, for more titles.

You can also find Joanne Rock on Facebook, along with other Harlequin Desire authors, at Facebook.com/harlequindesireauthors!

To Angela Anderson,
for uplifting everyone around you.
Thank you for all you do
to support the romance community!

One

Back in Jessamyn Barclay's Manhattan home, she had never once bumped into a former lover by accident. In that most densely populated of New York's five boroughs, it was a snap for her to avoid people she preferred not to see.

Now, she'd been standing inside Yampa Valley Regional Airport—gateway to Northwest Colorado according to the welcome sign—for all of ten minutes when she spied the one man whose path she did not wish to cross. Ryder Wakefield stood at the baggage claim carousel just one over from hers. And Ryder wasn't just any old boyfriend, either. He'd been the first man to show her what passion could be like.

And the one to win the prize for most damage

inflicted to her emotions. Even though he'd broken her heart as thoughtfully as possible.

Bastard. As if he'd thought she'd needed to be let down easily like some kind of fragile creature. Something Jessamyn Barclay had *never* been.

"Damn it." She darted behind a tall kid wearing a skateboard strapped to his back like a knapsack, hoping the excess baggage would hide her from Ryder's view.

For a minute, anyway. As vice president of a multinational real estate development company, she did not "hide" from anything. And it ticked her off to think how fast a sighting of Ryder turned back the clock and made her feel like a swoony teenager instead of the badass boss she'd become since then.

Peering around the lime-green skateboard painted with skulls, Jessamyn observed the man who had been one of many reasons she'd stayed away from the tiny town of Catamount, Colorado, for the past decade. He leaned with lazy grace against a cement column, his body packed with more lean muscle than she recalled. Broad shoulders stretched the fabric of his charcoal T-shirt. Her attention shifted lower despite herself, to where faded denim hugged heavy thighs.

She dragged her attention back to his face, where his angular cheekbones and square jaw were dusted with just enough whiskers to give a woman razor burn if…

Heat rushed through her as she halted that thought in its tracks. It didn't matter that she was a powerhouse executive now, the rainmaker for her father's real estate company, onboarding more clients and business than anyone else in the firm for three years running. Clearly, she'd maintained the hormones of her eighteen-year-old self. Ryder would turn heads in any city, and no amount of time or circumstance could change the fact that he was a ridiculously attractive man.

So Jessamyn decided to act like any self-respecting corporate shark. She pretended not to see him.

Tightening her grip on her handbag, a designer leather bucket purse as thoroughly out of its element as she was, Jessamyn focused on the baggage carousel in time to spot her suitcase. Her ticket out of this place, wedged firmly between a beat-up steamer trunk and an overstuffed duffel bag, inching her way at a snail's pace.

She darted past her skateboarder shield and edged around two older women in animated conversation. With an effort, she hauled the rose-gold case off the conveyor and onto the floor. Normally, she only traveled with a carry-on, well accustomed to expedient business travel. But she hadn't booked a return flight for this trip since she had no idea how long she'd stay in Catamount to finish settling her grandmother's affairs. Packing lightly hadn't been an option.

Her sister Fleur had gotten Jessamyn's promise to spend some time in their grandmother's house this summer. Time for memories before they sold the property off. That in itself had been a tough vow to make because Jessamyn had a strained relationship with both of her sisters ever since their parents' bitter divorce drew battle lines straight through the family.

For the first few years, she and her siblings had patched together enough of a bond to limp along. But even that tenuous connection had snapped almost a decade ago. If not for their grandmother's death and their shared inheritance of her ranch, the Crooked Elm, they would have happily continued going about their separate ways. Jessamyn suspected her grandmother had skipped leaving the property to her son to ensure the sisters would have to work together.

Wheeling her bag to the rental car kiosk, Jessamyn kept her focus on her target. Obtain the SUV she'd rented and begin the hour-long drive to Catamount. She needed to sort out her thoughts before she arrived at the ranch. Put her game face on for a conversation with Fleur. She couldn't afford a chink in her mental armor. Best to let her sister think she was still well-adjusted and thriving in their father's business even though Jessamyn was furious at Mateo Barclay for contesting their grandmother's will. Fleur hated their father, and Jessamyn refused to give her any leverage to pry apart the bond Jess had always had with their dad.

Somehow, she'd deal with all the other uncomfortable truths coming to the surface about their father. She loved him, and he'd believed in her when she'd felt like an outcast in her family—the only one who'd supported their dad. But these past few weeks had brought some issues to light.

"Barclay," she snapped at the young woman behind the rental kiosk a little more sharply than she'd intended. The stress of the past weeks had eaten away some of her poise. And then the near miss of running into Ryder... Amending her tone, she smiled politely. "I've got a luxury SUV reserved for the week, but I want to leave myself the option of extending the rental agreement."

Not that she was hiding out in Catamount, of course. No more than she'd been hiding from Ryder behind an unsuspecting traveler carrying a skateboard. But the same thinking applied here. Why borrow trouble? She didn't truly *need* to return to her office in midtown for the next few weeks, so why step back into her father's obvious power machinations too soon? Her stomach churned at the thought of the engagement announcement he was dying to make for her and her potential fiancé. The man Mateo had handpicked to be her husband and—not coincidentally—his successor at Barclay Property Group.

"Barclay?" The tall, reed-thin blonde in a red cardigan tapped her keys without enthusiasm. "I'll check, but we ran out of vehicles an hour ago."

"Excuse me?" Jessamyn leaned closer to the counter, all business. "I booked this a week ago. I have a reservation number." She turned the screen on her phone around so it faced the agent.

Tricia, according to the badge pinned to her lightweight sweater.

"There's a shortage," Tricia replied, her bland expression never changing as she consulted the monitor behind a clear partition. "We're out of vehicles."

In a major city, Jessamyn could have marched over to a competitor's counter. Or better yet, requested a car service that came with a driver so she could devote her full attention to shoring up her mental defenses before arriving at Crooked Elm. Here… what could she do?

While calling for an Uber would successfully deliver her home, it wouldn't solve the problem of how to get around town for the next week or two.

"What if I downgraded?" she suggested, worry pinching the spot between her eyebrows into a knot. "Took a smaller car?"

That got Tricia's attention. The agent looked up from her screen, her head tilting a fraction as she met Jessamyn's gaze. "We're out of vehicles of every size. If you'd like to leave your contact information, I can let you know when we get something in."

Anxiety stabbed her. Why hadn't she driven from Denver instead of taking that last little hop into Steamboat Springs to get closer to Catamount? Surely there were vehicles there. Should she look into flying back to the hub so she'd have a car at her disposal?

The thought of being pent up at Crooked Elm with no escape gave her that claustrophobic feeling she hadn't felt since the early days of her parents' divorce, when sharing a roof with any of the other Barclays could trigger panic episodes to the point of illness. Gulping for air, she tried to swallow the feeling as she glanced around the baggage area, buying herself some time to think.

Over at the other carousel, the crowd had diminished to just a couple of lingering passengers. Ryder was nowhere in sight, likely gone. A fact that eased her stress. A smidge.

Then again, it only put off the inevitable of seeing him again, something bound to happen in the tiny town he still called home. A fact confirmed for her on her last one-day trip when she and her father had flown in to attend Antonia Barclay's memorial service four weeks ago. Ryder had been there.

Thankfully, he'd left without seeking her out. Considering that behavior, maybe he'd also seen her today and had been content to pretend otherwise. The idea shouldn't bug her as much as it did. And damn, but she just wanted to get to Crooked Elm and sleep for the next three days. Between clearing her calendar for the next two weeks, her father's resentment that she wasn't giving in to his demands—and tossing in the thought of her potential marriage—it hadn't been an easy week. The tension between her eyes ratcheted tighter.

Turning back to the counter, she opened her lips to tell Tricia she'd find another way into Catamount when the other woman's expression brightened.

Transformed, really. The woman's pale eyes focused on a spot past Jessamyn's shoulder.

"I have your keys, Mr. Wakefield." The agent honest-to-God gave him a wink as she dug under the counter and withdrew a lumpy envelope.

Mr. Wakefield?

The hairs on the back of Jessamyn's neck rose, awareness and outrage mingling as she clocked the male presence at her back.

She didn't need to turn to know who stood behind her.

Still, her head swiveled around to glare at the man whose face had once dominated her every waking thought.

"How can *he* obtain a vehicle when I was here first?" Her eyes narrowed on Ryder's lazy smile.

His untroubled blue gaze swept over her briefly before returning to the rental car agent. "Thanks, Trish."

Before his fist could close over the packet, Jessamyn snatched it from the woman's hand.

"Excuse me?" She rounded on the agent, compressing her lips into a flat line while she attempted to rein herself in. She would not be *that* person in the airport taking out her frustrations on a customer service rep who was simply the face of their company's bottom-line-based decisions. And yet? She refused to be ignored in favor of a hot billionaire rancher. "This vehicle rightly belongs to me. I have a reservation. I am in front of this…" Searching for the right word took a moment, but she settled on something innocuous. And blatantly false. "…gentleman."

Tricia shook her head as she frowned at Jessamyn. "That's not one of our cars," she stated flatly.

Before the woman could continue, Ryder held up

a hand to forestall her words. "I've got this, Trish. Miss Barclay and I are old friends."

His icy glare was none-too-friendly despite the words. But then, he knew better than to try charming her. Not after the way they'd parted.

"Hello, Jessamyn. Nice to see you again." He spoke the words like a performance art piece. All for show. No emotion.

His hard jaw flexed in a way that hollowed out his cheeks and drew her attention to his sculpted lips. It really was annoying how handsome he was. She huffed out an angry breath.

"Hardly. And before you ask, no, we can't share the ride." She shoved the heavy envelope into her bucket purse, taking full possession of the rental vehicle. Never taking her eyes off him, she addressed the agent, "Tricia, can you tell me what I'll be driving today so I can sign the paperwork and be on my way?"

Ryder's lips quirked up on one side, almost as if she amused him. Would he be amused to cool his heels in the airport for a few hours while she left him eating her dust?

"Those are the keys to Mr. Wakefield's Tesla," Tricia informed her from behind the counter. "His *personal* vehicle."

It took a moment for the words to sink in after Jessamyn had been so sure she'd bested him. Could what she was saying be true?

Ryder's mouth curved even more, threatening a

full-blown grin. Jessamyn dove a hand into her bag to extract the envelope and ripped it open.

Inside, she found a shiny black fob in the shape of a vehicle with no key attached at all. Along with it, however, there was a folded note with the name Ryder scratched across the outside of the paper in a spare, masculine hand.

"My brother dropped it off for me at the airport last night," Ryder informed her, taking the fob and the note from her hands. The warmth of his touch sent a buzz through her skin in a way that proved even more humiliating than the misunderstanding over the car.

Before she could reply, he lowered his voice for her ears alone, leaning closer to say, "And since I'm far more gracious than you, Jessie, you can share my ride anytime."

Ryder could practically hear her spitting nails as she followed him into the now-deserted airport drop-off area a few minutes later. Only about thirty flights went through the regional facility in a day, and theirs must have been the last two. Since they'd lingered in the baggage area well after everyone else had found rides home, there was no one else around to hear her tirade about men who thought the rest of the world existed to do their bidding.

"...and since when is the local car rental shop the Wakefield family valet service?" Her high heels clicked in time to her rapid-fire words as she dogged his steps away from the terminal and into the small parking lot surrounded by green fields on all sides.

He didn't need to look behind him to know she pulled her rose-gold suitcase with her. The wheels rolled over the tarmac with a constant drone. He'd offered to carry the bag for her, and she'd only yanked it closer to her side in answer.

Ten years had changed a lot about Jessamyn Barclay, but she remained as prickly and independent as ever.

She was also still smoking hot.

Now Ryder turned on his heel to answer her most recent question. "Since Tricia is my niece."

She nearly slammed into him, pulling to a halt at the last second and tilting her chin to meet his gaze.

Hazel eyes more green than brown blinked back at him, her lush dark hair beginning to pull loose from a twist she'd secured with a clip. She wore a taupe-colored suit that skimmed her curves like it never wanted to let go, the pencil skirt stopping just above her knee while the jacket hugged a white silk tank top that molded to perfect-sized breasts. The outfit looked as expensive as the rest of her. From the high heels that would serve no purpose on her family's ranch in the western Rockies to the even more impractical suitcase, she broadcast the cosmopolitan polish she'd sought when she left Catamount ten years before.

"Your niece," she repeated, her full lips twisting to one side as if to chew that over. "That's why she winked when she called you Mr. Wakefield. I sup-

pose you are reaping the benefits of small-town life."
There was a grudging acknowledgment in her tone.

Her gaze lifted to look beyond him, roaming over
the mountain view in the distance before returning to
the cornfield nearby. Did she find any aspect of that
vista enjoyable? She'd been so hell-bent on leaving
this place once upon a time. But he knew how a town
like Catamount could suck you back in. After their
parents retired from ranching and moved to Phoe-
nix, Ryder's older brother had given up his share of
the family ranch to marry his college sweetheart in
Idaho. Yet Trey still visited Catamount year after
year, and his college-aged daughter picked up summer jobs in Steamboat Springs.

Ryder had taken advantage of the opportunities
outside this remote corner of Northwestern Colorado, but he always returned home.

"It's absolutely a perk. As is being able to arrive
in the airport and find someone you know to give
you a lift home," he reminded her, the doors unlock-
ing as he neared his vehicle.

She glanced at the car, as if surprised to see they'd
arrived at his ride.

"I really shouldn't," she began quietly, as if talking to herself.

That ticked him off. Bad enough she'd wanted
to act like she hadn't even recognized him inside
the airport. Yeah, he'd noticed. He'd decided to let
it pass because he'd been the one to blame for their
breakup. Didn't matter that it had been a decade ago,
when they were both barely adults. Their connection

had been real enough, and it had hurt him like hell to send her away. He'd bet anything that he'd hurt her, too. So he'd bear the weight of being the bad guy in that scenario.

But for her to play games with him about a ride home, when they were both heading to the same place? He'd be damned if he'd be her personal scapegoat for all the things that irritated Jessamyn Barclay.

"Why is that?" He edged fractionally closer. Just enough to break the barrier of her personal space. "Afraid the old chemistry is still there?"

Even as he asked, he felt the electric pulse of it leap from her flashing hazel eyes into his skin. Awareness throbbed in his veins, multiplying like a virus he couldn't shake.

Yet Jessamyn's bottom lip curled as if she found the very idea offensive. Maybe the attraction felt like a virus on her end, too.

"Definitely not." She nearly snarled the words, leaving the pointed edges on them.

"Then what's got you all worked up about riding home with me?" He raised the trunk, then lowered his bag and climbing gear into the back. He waited to see if Jessamyn would make the trip with him.

Frowning, she folded her arms and shot back, "I am hardly *worked up*, Ryder. I'm just wondering how I'll go about obtaining a rental if I leave here without one."

He could see her point. Catamount wasn't much more than a map dot.

"Fleur has a vehicle," he mused aloud, thinking

through the problem. "I've seen her delivering baked goods to the Cowboy Kitchen some mornings. Aren't you staying with her?"

"I can't just borrow my sister's car. Especially when she clearly needs it." Her grip tightened on the handle of her shiny suitcase, one manicured nail tapping thoughtfully.

His attention drifted over her again, lingering on one cocked hip where the fabric of her skirt stretched to accommodate the movement. An old memory returned with sudden vividness—him pulling her closer by her hips. Her melting against him and twining her arms around his neck.

They were a long way from those days, he reminded himself, cranking his head up to meet her gaze again.

"But she could probably give you a lift back here when they have a car available." He wanted to get on the road, damn it, not argue with a woman who belonged in his past. "Do you want a ride or not? I can't hang around here shooting the breeze all day."

She only hesitated a moment before she gave a clipped nod.

"Yes, please." She smacked the retractable handle on her fancy luggage back into place, then moved to lift the bag herself.

Stifling his own tirade about hardheaded women, Ryder took the heavy bag from her and slid it into the trunk before closing the lift gate.

Jessamyn remained silent as he opened the passenger door and helped her in, then went around the

vehicle to take his own seat. He'd known for weeks—
ever since Antonia Barclay's death—that Jessamyn
would most likely show up in town again.

Until a few days ago, he'd expected they'd do their
best to avoid each other. As they had since their long-
ago summer relationship. Then Ryder heard through
the grapevine that her father was contesting Antonia's will—a will that left the Crooked Elm Ranch to
her three granddaughters, including Jessamyn. Ryder
had his reasons for not wanting to be involved with
any of the Barclays, let alone the woman he'd briefly
hoped for a future with. But if Mateo Barclay per-
sisted in barring Jessamyn from inheriting the ranch
that should rightfully be hers, Ryder knew he'd have
no choice but to share information he'd safeguarded
for nine long years.

For now, however, he'd bide his time. Pulling out
of the airport parking lot and onto the main road,
Ryder reminded himself that Jess would likely iron
things out on her own. He couldn't imagine anyone
shortchanging her from what she believed should be
rightfully hers. So Ryder wouldn't have any reason
to interfere in her affairs.

No reason at all to see her elegant curves and
smoking-hot stares again.

He'd just about firmed up that plan in his mind,
when Jessamyn's silky voice wound through the
plush black interior of his vehicle.

"Now who's worked up?" she asked mildly.

He slanted a glance her way. "Me? I haven't said
a word since we got in the car."

"That's exactly how I can tell you're annoyed." She shifted in the seat, as if she was settling in for an interrogation. "I snipe when I'm irritated. You go silent. Is it because I said you had the world to do your bidding?" she mused aloud as she adjusted the air-conditioning vent to blow toward her face.

Her neck.

She plucked the silk fabric of her tank away from her skin just below her collarbone, the action dragging his attention to her breasts and the body-hugging jacket that framed them.

And shouldn't his eyes be on the road? He whipped his head around, grateful there was no traffic to speak of in this part of town. Green fields lay on either side of them as he drove west toward Catamount.

"It's been ten years since we've seen each other. You really think you know me well enough to guess what I'm thinking anymore?"

She scoffed at that, letting go of her blouse and sinking into the seat. "*You* suggested I was afraid of potential chemistry." The word dripped with disdain. "It sounds like you think we're both stuck in the past."

"Touché." He nodded, granting her the point even as he tried to recall the last time he'd had her in his passenger seat. Their history together had been brief but intense, the memories of their touches imprinted on his brain. His body. "So we've established there's no longer any attraction between us, and also that you don't know what I'm thinking." He wasn't sure about either one, but he didn't want to argue with her the whole car ride home. "Any suggestions for conversational topics to fill the void for the fifty-minute ride we're looking at? Are we relegated to commenting on the weather? Making polite inquiries about each other's jobs?"

Jessamyn picked at the button on her jacket cuff, a single gold bangle sliding down her wrist. "I'm sure you don't want to discuss my latest real estate deal any more than I care to hear about your high-tech ranch upgrades."

He raised an eyebrow at that, wondering how she knew about the changes he'd made at his ranch. Had she been keeping tabs on him? The awareness she refused to acknowledge sparked to life, warming the air between them.

How long had it been since he'd tasted her? The question made him very aware of the two years it had been since his last relationship ended. He'd been too busy with the ranch to date, a fact that hadn't bothered him much until today, when the sudden, sharp desire for the woman next to him was the last thing he needed.

"All right, then." He couldn't quite keep the gratified note out of his voice.

"I've got a conversational topic anyway," she rushed to add, sitting up straighter. Uncrossing her long legs, she put both feet on the floor mat. "In the interest of making sure you believe me that the chemistry is thoroughly dead, I can tell you about my future husband."

Two

The silence stretched.

Jessamyn watched Ryder steer the vehicle along Route 40 heading west, following the Yampa River toward Catamount. The scenery outside the car was flat and green, an empty train track snaking alongside the road. The view inside the sleek black sports coupe proved far more compelling.

Ryder's jaw ticked, a pulse throbbing there even though nothing of the rest of him moved. Even his hands were still, the highway unfurling in an easy line for miles ahead.

"Future husband? As in this guy needs to be coerced into proposing?" Cool blue eyes flicked her way before returning to the lane in front of him. "I sure as hell don't see a ring on your finger."

Glancing at her bare left hand on the armrest, she yanked it out of sight, tucking her fingers under her thigh. As soon as she'd done it, of course, she felt the flush of awkward embarrassment.

Sort of like bringing up her almost husband in the first place. How come she could play it cool with any other man in the world but this one? She'd been in his car for less than ten minutes, and she'd already reverted to the starry-eyed girl she'd once been.

"It's not official yet," she forced herself to say calmly, feigning indifference when she was actually tense as hell about the whole engagement question. She really needed to get her head on straight while she was in Catamount. "There's been no rush to announce our partnership since it will have implications at Barclay Property Group. We thought we'd save it for our next investor meeting."

She'd proposed the timeline to her father, hoping to gain some breathing room for her and Brandon to get on the same page before making an engagement official. After all these years, she'd never felt the passion she'd had with Ryder. And she'd come to believe that looking at marriage as something practical rather than romantic would be the key to success.

They'd both been too busy to date much, so taking their relationship from co–vice presidents to something romantic would require time and effort. In the meantime, her father couldn't wait to unveil Barclay's new "power couple."

"You've got to be kidding me." Ryder shook his head, sliding the fingers of one hand through his dark hair while he anchored the steering wheel with the other. "You're going to make your marriage a business decision?"

"On the contrary, I'm using my marriage announcement to further my business goals." Not that she owed him an explanation. For some reason, she resented Brandon's willingness to treat their future relationship as a business deal, even if that was her own rationalization. But the impending engagement was on her mind. And if she could use it to forestall thoughts of the man sitting beside her, all the better. "There's nothing wrong with being judicious about sharing aspects of my personal life in a way that will help my career."

"Sure there is. It's called selling out. And it's cold as hell. Too cold for a marriage." He slanted another hard look her way before his attention snagged briefly on something beyond her.

Following his gaze, she spotted a group of mule deer in the field. Two of them looked up at the car as it passed, their big ears twitching. She turned her attention back to Ryder as he passed a slow-moving hay truck towing stacked bales.

"Spoken like a man who's never had to think twice about balancing a personal and a professional life." Stabbing the button to lower the window, she inhaled the scent of green grass and trees mingled with a hint of the river. She didn't allow herself to miss Colorado very often, but the larger-than-life landscape had always pulled at her.

"Only because I don't have a personal life," he

admitted. "With my parents retired and my brother off in Idaho, I don't spend much time with family. Even though I see Trish more these days, there's still a distance." Was there a hint of regret in his tone? She barely had time to weigh the words before he lowered his voice to a silky octave. "Didn't anyone ever tell you that business and pleasure don't mix?"

She'd be lying if she said the word *pleasure* tripping off his tongue in that particular tone didn't stir something deep in the pit of her belly. Good thing she had the news of her impending engagement to keep those feelings at bay.

Fighting the urge to both fan herself and check her watch to see how many more minutes they would be enclosed in this small space together, Jessamyn shifted in her seat.

"My business *is* a pleasure." She hit the button to raise her window again, then reached for the air-conditioning vent to point it at her overheated face.

She'd always loved the challenge of her job, closing real estate deals and being a part of groundbreaking new developments. But for the past eighteen months she'd been questioning her professional future. Would the same type of work make her happy forever? Maybe once she and Brandon took over the business, it would feel different. More personal.

"That's good to hear. I remember how much you dreamed of being where you are now." He eased the car around a bend in the road as they began heading south. Gentle hills hinted at the more mountainous terrain ahead, where they'd skirt the north of the Flat Tops Wilderness before reaching Catamount.

"Climbing the ranks at my father's company has been rewarding. He has encouraged my relationship with Brandon and our goals for the business," she said carefully, unwilling to think about the dreams she'd once confided to Ryder. Dreams that had her working out West in real estate instead of New York. But she would not be trekking down memory lane with him on this trip. So she reached for any other topic, seizing on the first thing that came into her brain. "What brought you to the airport today? Have you been out of town long?"

"I was in the Alaska Panhandle doing climbing of another kind for the last ten days. But I needed to come home to oversee some modifications to my house." He slowed for a group of cyclists pedaling hard as they bent over their handlebars. "I'm refitting the main home to run off solar and wind power only."

Impressive. She couldn't deny it.

"My grandmother mentioned that to me in our last phone conversation." She swallowed past the grief that still came when she thought of how long it had been since she'd seen her grandmother in person.

"I'm sorry for your loss. I know how much you cared for her," Ryder assured her quietly. "I missed you at the memorial, but you were on my mind that day."

The sincerity behind the words reminded her of what she'd once liked most about this man. She'd thought him the kindest person she'd ever met.

Until…he hadn't been. She pressed the heel of her hand to her sternum as a pain sprang up there.

She resented the physical manifestations of her emotions that made her feel out of control. Was this what her mother had felt like when she'd battled depression after her divorce? Shaking off the empathy that her mother had never wanted from her, Jessamyn stared out the window.

Ryder passed the next group of bikers, picking up speed as the sun sank lower, casting the sky in shades of pink and violet.

"I— That is, thank you." She'd only flown in for the day of the service. Knowing the sisters had lost the chance to reconcile in the presence of the grandmother who'd wanted that more than anything had lit a fire under Jessamyn. She'd vowed to get her personal life together.

With her estranged siblings, for starters. But also with her lackluster romantic life. She'd taken her father's suggestion of marrying more seriously after Antonia's death. At least Brandon understood the demands on her professional life. They could build on that. Craft a future that wasn't full of tension and combat, like her parents' marriage.

"Did your future husband make the trip with you?" Ryder asked, tone cooling.

"No. I attended with my father, which seemed fitting." She wouldn't try explaining her relationship to Ryder since she wasn't sure he'd understand the appeal of a partner who was more a friend and teammate than a romantic attachment.

"In other words, your boyfriend sat at home in New York while you mourned one of the most significant people in your life." His grip tightened on the steering wheel as they wound through steeper hills, trees crowding closer to the car. "I don't mean to judge, Jess—"

"It sure sounds like you're judging," she shot back, crossing her legs and her arms, shifting in her seat to look out the passenger window.

Of all the people she could have possibly caught a ride with today, why did it have to be a former love? A man who could still get under her skin?

"I just hope you'll give the engagement some thought while you're in town. Marriage is a big step."

She hated that he gave her advice she'd already been planning to take. It made it tougher to argue.

"Is that why you've never taken the plunge? Not all of us can afford to wait for life to be perfect before making a commitment." As soon as the words were out there, she realized how much they smacked of sour grapes. As if she were still smarting over his dismissal of her love ten years ago. Which was laughable. So laughable, in fact, that she turned the topic to something neutral. "Tell me more about your changes. Antonia said there was a yurt?"

If Ryder noticed that she'd fallen back on the topic of conversation that she'd said earlier she wasn't interested in, he didn't comment on it. Maybe he was as eager to leave behind the more sensitive subject as she was.

With any luck, Ryder's discussion of his off-thegrid house would take them the rest of the way to Catamount. She wouldn't have to think about his objections to her future fiancé, or the fact that she might feel the smallest amount of chemistry around Ryder after all.

She knew, of course, what lay down that path since she'd already foolishly followed it. Following her personal passions hadn't paid off, so she'd find romantic happiness another way.

This time, she'd thank Ryder for the ride home and then there'd be no reason in the world to see him again while she was in town.

He *had* to see her again.

Four days after dropping Jessamyn in front of the Crooked Elm Ranch, Ryder stood in line at the Cowboy Kitchen, the only restaurant in the small town of Catamount. At 6 a.m., the breakfast rush was on as locals vied for the best pick of fresh baked goods handmade by Fleur Barclay, Jess's younger sister. Fleur, a professional chef, had turned the Cowboy Kitchen into a morning hot spot since her arrival in Catamount last month. She'd started out making pastries and muffins at the Crooked Elm to sell at the eatery, but over time she'd gotten close to Drake Alexander, a local rancher and owner of the restaurant. Rumor had it Fleur was poised to take over the place and expand the business.

From his spot in the queue behind a crusty old rancher in overalls, Ryder could see copper-haired Fleur loading more pastries into the glass bakery case perched on the old diner counter. He'd caught glimpses of Jessamyn in the background, carrying trays and bakery boxes to give her sister a hand.

Just as he'd hoped. He'd mentally regrouped since their encounter at the airport, and he recognized that he needed to speak to her about her grandmother's will.

Sooner rather than later. The possibility that he was sitting on information that could help her in defending her grandmother's wishes was eating away at him. Hence his morning visit to the Cowboy Kitchen. His foreman was a regular here, bringing pastries back to the ranch at least twice a week, and he'd mentioned that Fleur's sister had been helping her recently.

"Next!" Marta Macon, the cheery brunette who served as both a hostess and server, called from her spot at the register, her silver name tag glinting under the counter's pendant lighting.

The line shuffled forward even as the front bell chimed behind him, signaling another customer arriving. The decor remained the same as ever— white countertops, black-and-white laminate floors, chrome barstools with turquoise seats from a bygone era. An oversize painting of a faded brown Stetson hung on the wall above the counter. Although Ryder suspected the look of the place would be changing soon with Fleur Barclay on the scene.

Except Fleur wasn't the woman who'd captured his attention this morning. Jessamyn carried out yet another tray of baked goods from a seemingly endless supply in the kitchen. She wore a white chef's apron cinched around her narrow waist, with her dark, glossy hair clipped high at the back of her head. The tennis shoes on her feet instead of high heels added to the contrast of her airport outfit. And when she turned her back to the counter, Ryder could see a pair of jean shorts and a cropped tee that had been hiding behind that industrial apron.

A hint of thigh was just visible from his vantage point on the other side of the counter before Marta shouted again, "Next!" Then, recognizing him, the woman curved her lips into a wide smile. "Hi, Ryder. Should I get your usual?"

Jessamyn whirled around at the mention of his name, her hazel eyes homing in on him with a faintly accusing air.

Just looking at her, he found his body stirring despite everything—being in public, being on the receiving end of Jess's obvious displeasure, and needing to give his breakfast order.

"Sure thing, but can you double it today? I'm meeting a friend." He allowed his gaze to return to Jessamyn, who scowled at him briefly before pivoting away to charge into the kitchen.

He tried not to follow the twitch of her hips in those denim cutoffs, but that proved a losing battle.

"Of course," Marta answered with her usual enthusiasm, reading him his total and making change before she continued. "I'm excited about the Atlas Gala at Wakefield Ranch later this month. Congratulations on the Captain Earth Award."

He tried not to cringe at the title worthy of a comic-book hero instead of a rancher trying to do what was best for his land with sustainable development. He knew the Atlas Foundation's goal was to draw attention to their mission of protecting the planet, and if the kitschy name of an award helped them garner headlines, all the better.

"Thank you. I'm glad to hear you'll be at the gala." He slid the change into the tip jar and stepped out of the way to wait for his coffees, already wondering how he could intercept Jessamyn.

A moment later, a white paper bag and two coffees in hand, Ryder stepped outside into the parking lot in front of the Cowboy Kitchen. He'd spotted Fleur's vehicle on the way into the restaurant, so he had an advantage for knowing where Jessamyn might retreat.

Sure enough, she was already in the passenger seat of the silver rattletrap that Fleur had driven into Catamount last month. Ryder knew Drake Alexander was in the market to replace it for her, since his friend had approached him about an extra truck that Ryder kept in his equipment barn for emergencies. He would have sold it to him, too, but Fleur had wanted the satisfaction of purchasing her own vehicle.

Catching Jessamyn's eye, he held the bakery bag up in front of the windshield.

"Hungry?" he asked through the tempered glass.

Slowly, her window lowered via a hand crank.

Her hair was down now, loose around her shoulders, and she'd removed her apron so that she sat in the passenger seat in her faded red crop top and frayed jean shorts. The white edges of the denim blew along her skin as the morning breeze filtered into the car, the outfit a far cry from the sleek, expensive outfit she'd worn in the airport four days ago. Right now, she looked like the Jessamyn he remembered from a decade ago.

"I thought you were meeting someone for breakfast?" One elegant eyebrow lifted in question.

Only now, seeing her up close in the morning sunlight, did he spot the violet smudges under her eyes. Had she been losing sleep?

He passed her a coffee, hoping like hell that her grandmother's will hadn't been the source of anxiety. "That someone is you. Can you spare some time this morning?"

When she seemed to hesitate, not accepting his offering, he pressed his case.

"We need to talk. And when I left the restaurant, I noticed your sister deep in conversation with Drake Alexander. So if you're waiting for her, it could be a while before she joins you."

Jessamyn huffed out a sigh. "Once they step into each other's orbits, it's like the whole rest of the world ceases to exist." Was there a wistful note in her voice? For a moment, he wondered about that fiancé of hers if Jessamyn didn't know that same kind of gravitational pull Drake and Fleur had for each other. Before Ryder could dwell on that, she rolled up the window and pushed open the car door to step outside. "Even so, I probably wouldn't have said yes if not for the coffee."

"Cream only, no sugar," he informed her as she took the cup, her fingers brushing his briefly.

He noticed a bandage on the back of her hand as hazel eyes darted to his over the rim.

"Good memory," she murmured, sounding surprised. "Thank you."

Her praise, however small, shouldn't feel so damned good. He shook off the warmth she'd stirred inside him, reminding himself he'd sought her out for a reason, and it wasn't to indulge an old attraction, no matter how tempting that might be.

"What happened to your hand?" He pointed to the bandage, curious how she'd been spending her time for the past few days.

"Spider bite. I've been sorting through some things in Gran's attic." She took a sip of the drink, her eyes closing appreciatively.

His gaze stalled on her long lashes fanned over her cheeks, some of her tension obviously easing as she enjoyed the coffee. He decided then and there he wanted to do more things to put that expression of pleasure on her face again. Then, recalling her words, he cautioned, "I hope you had that looked at. Some spiders can be dangerous around here."

"I did a telehealth visit. It's all good." She leaned against the car's trunk, and he recalled his ulterior motive.

"Would you mind if we take the food on the road?" He pointed toward his work truck, an old gray 4x4. "You can text Fleur that you're with me, and I'll drop you off at the ranch afterward."

For a moment, she seemed to weigh this. Was she thinking about that man in her life again? The thought ticked him off and at the same time made him all the more determined to convince her. He shouldn't care this much, yet he didn't have a chance of telling himself it didn't matter.

At her nod, relief rushed through him. He started walking toward his pickup, not giving her time to change her mind. He could hear her dictating a message into her phone as he opened the passenger door for her and assumed she was letting her sister know they were together.

A few minutes later, they were underway. Ryder headed toward a spot he frequented in the mornings when he needed time away from the ranch. Trying not to dwell on the vision Jessamyn's bare legs made where she stretched them into the footwell, he focused on his reason for seeking her out. Before he could launch into the subject that was likely to shut her down, she cleared her throat to speak.

"The suspense is killing me," she announced, planting an elbow on the truck's armrest as she tracked the rolling hills outside. "What gives with the private conversation? Especially when we had all the time in the world to talk just a few days ago?"

She'd never been one to mince words. Back when they were dating, he'd liked that about Jessamyn Barclay. He'd trusted her to be forthright. Honest. But right now, when he wrestled with his moral obligation to protect privacy as a rescue worker versus information he believed she should know, that candid quality in her made him conflicted. Uneasy.

Should he come right out and tell her he was in a dicey situation with proprietary information he wasn't at liberty to share, even though it could help her with the battle over the will? Or would that only turn up the heat on him to spill what he knew?

"I heard your father is contesting Antonia's will," he said carefully. "I always considered your grandmother a friend, and if there's any way I can help, I want you to know that you and your sisters have my support."

"That's what this is about?" She pivoted in her seat to face him, her legs shifting in a way that drew his attention despite himself. "The will?"

"Not just the will, Jess. It's about Crooked Elm and your grandmother's wishes. I know she wanted you and your sisters to have the ranch one day."

"She told you that?"

"Not in so many words, but it was obvious in the way she spoke—" He cut himself off when he realized she was shaking her head. "What is it? You don't agree?"

"Of course I agree. But a belief or hearsay isn't likely to help us in court." Abruptly, she leaned forward to point out the windshield. "Hey. Isn't this the bridge near your ranch?"

The truck trundled over the wooden structure he'd rebuilt two years ago.

"I was wondering when you'd notice where we

were headed." He was glad for the reprieve in the conversation. He needed to think about what evidence he could offer first. Gather more information. "You mentioned the yurt on the ride from the airport. I figured we could have breakfast here."

He hoped she wouldn't mind that he'd brought her here. Some of their history was tied to his ranch. They'd shared a memorable first kiss on the old bridge that had spanned the waterway he'd just crossed.

Sneaking a sideways glance at her, he caught her furrowed brow as her gaze swept the horizon. Without his permission, his attention dipped briefly to her full mouth. Her tongue swept along the upper lip in a brief swipe that had his groin tightening.

Thankfully, their destination appeared around the next bend, breaking the moment.

"Oh, wow," she breathed, a note of awe in her voice as she took in the octagonal structure set in a wooded corner of his property. "It's beautiful."

Parking the truck nearby, Ryder hoped he hadn't made a mistake in bringing her here. He'd hoped he could draw her out about where things stood with her grandmother's will.

But as he shut off the ignition and gathered up the white bags with their breakfast, he was very aware of the old attraction that still simmered between them. When Jessamyn unfastened her seat belt and peered up at him from under long lashes, he could feel that she was every bit as conscious of the chemistry as he was.

Grinding his molars against the awareness jolting through him, he decided he just needed to get through this conversation and a shared meal. Then he'd have the answers he needed, and he could leave Jessamyn Barclay to her own devices until she returned to New York and her not-quite fiancé who clearly wasn't worthy of her.

Yet as he moved around to the passenger side of the truck to help her down to the ground, just one touch of her hand in his sent enough sparks through him to assure him he was lying through his teeth.

Three

How was it possible that Ryder's gaze aroused her more than any other man's touch? And more importantly, how was she going to keep her desire hidden through their breakfast? In the past week, she'd exchanged a few texts with Brandon, but they'd mostly involved work and potential public appearances. No thought of Brandon had stirred her so.

As the compelling rancher followed her to the inviting outdoor structure, Jessamyn could swear she felt his gunmetal-blue gaze on her skin as surely as a fingertip trailing up her spine. Awareness pricked along the back of her neck, raising goose bumps on her arms while she wove her way toward the glass-and-wood building reflecting the morning sunlight.

Two decks wrapped around the back, only partially

visible from where she stood. One deck sprawled out at ground level, with a firepit and cushioned deck chairs. The other had been raised as if to access an interior loft. Nearby, a brook—a feeder stream for the White River—babbled, but the soothing sound did little to settle her nerves. She'd walked beside the creek with Ryder once, and they'd paused on the arch of the wooden bridge when they'd kissed for the first time.

Was it just nostalgia and old memories making her heart pound now? Or was the attraction she felt a current, living thing? The buzz in her veins sure seemed vibrant. Fresh.

Persistent.

His voice rumbled from behind her. "Do you mind if we sit outside to eat?"

The sound of him—closer than she'd expected—sent an empty ache through her midsection.

She told herself it must be hunger for food. She just needed sustenance, right?

"That would be good," she agreed, her voice husky. Clearing her throat, she stepped onto a raised platform that wrapped around the yurt, following the planks to the back deck. "And then I want to see inside. I'm curious about why you'd build a yurt instead of—I don't know—a hunting cabin?"

He laughed, and for a moment, she let his good mood warm hers.

"For starters, City Girl, I'm too close to my own livestock for hunting." He swiped a broad palm over the cushion of one of the patio chairs, chasing away a few fallen leaves. His broad shoulders stretched the fabric of the black button-down shirt. Then he held the chair out to her. "Have a seat."

"Thank you," she murmured, lowering herself onto the plump gray cushion. A view of the mountains was framed between two tall pines some twenty yards from the deck. The effect was like looking at a three-dimensional painting. "And I do realize you wouldn't hunt this close to your grazing fields. I haven't been in New York long enough to forget my family's roots. I only meant that a yurt seemed like a surprising choice for a ranch outbuilding."

Breathing in the scent of cedar and juniper, she waited while Ryder withdrew pastries from the bags and laid them on paper napkins he arranged on the low wooden table between their chairs. Two chocolate croissants. Two *xuixos*, deep-fried and sugar-crusted confections that originated in Catalonia, Spain, the recipe arriving in Catamount via Antonia Barclay. Fleur loved baking all her grandmother's recipes, especially tapas and Spanish-inspired pastries.

"I'm hoping to rent this out for guests who enjoy ecotourism but still want a taste of ranch life." He pried the top from his coffee and took a long swallow.

Jessamyn's gaze followed the move, her eyes snagging on the hollow at the base of his throat. With an effort, she tried to conjure up an image of Brandon's face to ward off Ryder's magnetic draw.

She couldn't. Instead, she scavenged her brain to follow the conversation.

"Ecotourism? I thought that meant traveling to wilderness areas and leaving them undisturbed." Taking a big bite of the *xuixo* that she'd helped her sister bake at 3 a.m., Jessamyn hoped a sugar fix would ease the hunger for the man next to her.

"Initially, that's how the term was used. But in a broader sense today, travelers are looking for ways to see the world and use less resources while they do. I'm trying to make Wakefield Ranch a destination of interest for people who are curious about sustainable living."

She recalled the conversation she'd caught snippets of earlier at the Cowboy Kitchen and smothered a grin. "I may have overheard something about the Captain Earth Award."

Even as she teased him, she also had to admit his efforts were admirable.

A couple of friendly gray jays landed nearby and hopped closer, perhaps sensing the possibility of an easy meal.

"It's a publicity tactic for the conservation group, but I can hardly complain when they're making inroads with a younger demographic." Ryder tore off a corner of his pastry and tossed it to the pair of songbirds. "Next door to Crooked Elm, Drake is already working to restore wetlands along the river. I'm complementing the effort here to show how a ranch can work harmoniously with the environment."

"I'm impressed," she admitted honestly, watching the little jays squawk over their treat as they pecked it into bird-sized bits. "But I know that's not why you wanted to talk to me. You said you were willing to help me with my case against my father, but I'm not sure how you can."

Ryder shook his head, scowling. "I just don't understand why he would do that to you in the first place. He knew what your grandmother intended."

Tensing, she bristled at the accusation in his voice. "Wrongheaded as he may be, I'm sure he has our interests at heart." She needed to believe that. "He said he's concerned Lark and Fleur will outvote whatever I want to do with the property. He hopes to even the odds if he has a voice."

Even though she defended her dad, on the inside, she was still furious with him over it. His explanation implied that, even if he lost the case to have himself declared the primary beneficiary of the will, he would still try to obtain a portion of the estate equal to Jessamyn's and her sisters'. How could he have thought that would honor his mother's wishes?

Ryder set aside his coffee, his pastry finished. Then, he pivoted to face her full on.

"Do you believe what he said about putting your needs first?" Those cool blue eyes probed hers, seeing right through to her thoughts.

"He's given me good guidance in the past," she answered, hedging. "My career has taken off because of him."

"It's taken off because of *you*, Jess. Don't avoid the question. Do you truly believe he's looking out for you now?"

She itched to ask why it mattered to him enough

to bring her here to quiz her about it. But between the concern in his eyes—for her—and the fact that she worried about this issue, too, she thought maybe she owed it to herself to answer him honestly.

"No, I don't," she confessed, agitated and feeling disloyal about having to admit her doubts. "But *he* believes it, Ryder. I'm sure of that much."

His jaw flexed, the muscle working silently as he seemed to chew that over.

"So you'll admit he doesn't know what's best for you with your grandmother's ranch," he pressed, leaning closer to lay a gentle hand on her forearm. Pushing into her personal space. "How could you believe he'd ever know what you need in a husband?"

Her mouth dried up.

At his touch. His nearness.

His unexpected counterattack on the question of her potential engagement.

A hundred responses circled through her brain. That it was none of his damned business. That Ryder didn't know what he was talking about any more than her father did with regard to her personal life. But the only reply she wanted to make was a silent press of her lips to Ryder's firm, sculpted mouth.

She wanted that so much, in fact, she shoved to her feet to escape his nearness. Escape the tangible seduction of his gaze sliding over her.

Striding to the low fence surrounding the deck, Jessamyn gripped the smooth wood handrail, her nails biting into the surface.

"I like and respect Brandon. I agreed to the match

based on our common goals and interests." Even as she said it, she knew Brandon's proposal was never going to happen now.

If she couldn't even conjure up a vision of her potential life partner's face while Ryder was around, then she was doing herself—and Brandon—a huge disservice to even consider saying yes. She couldn't build a personal partnership with someone who didn't share her vision of the future, nor could she raise a family with a man who didn't share her aspirations. The loss of that dream, even if it had been a foolish one, raked out her insides, leaving her empty of everything save the heated awareness of Ryder as he left his patio chair to stand behind her.

"You can't sacrifice personal happiness for someone who checks a bunch of boxes." The warmth of his chest blocked the breeze from her back, the cedar-and-leather scent of him stealing around her as surely as a touch. "It's a bloodless way to approach a relationship."

The words rattled her even as she battled the old awareness for Ryder, a live-wire connection that had never been fully shut down.

"Bloodless?" As she spun around to face him, the word was a quiet whisper rasping up her dry throat. It held a world of ghosts in it for them, the echo of a long-ago argument returned from the dead. "You think I don't feel? That I make decisions like some kind of automaton?"

She felt the warmth of his breath on her face, the force of his frustration with her. Those gunmetal-blue eyes sparked with an internal fire, the silver streaks near his pupils turning molten.

"Don't you?"

The challenge stung like a gauntlet to her cheek.

An answering anger rushed through her, tangling up with the desire held in check for too long. Her hand fisted in the placket of his black button-down shirt before she could consider what she was doing.

"How dare you?" She vibrated with each slam of her heartbeat against her ribs, as if that vital organ wanted to get closer to Ryder, too. "I feel. I have the same hungers coursing through my veins as you."

The force of them made her feel light-headed. Dizzy with awareness of this man and all the things they'd once felt for each other.

Even so, she told herself to walk away. To relax her grip on his shirt and pull it together.

But at the same moment, Ryder's mouth descended toward hers. Gently. Slowly.

Giving her time to choose what she wanted. That searing gaze checked in with hers as he neared, seeing what she wanted. Gauging her reaction.

Something about that combination of raw attraction and his cautious approach undid her. Like he'd reached inside her and seen exactly what she needed. Craved.

When his lips finally brushed over hers, she allowed the electric spark to open a circuit between them, the current of need fusing their months together.

Had he goaded her into the kiss?

The fear circled around Ryder's brain, warning

him he needed to break the connection. He couldn't allow an impulsive moment to give Jessamyn any reason to feel regret later.

Just one more minute.

After ten years without tasting her, he couldn't let her go just yet. Not until he'd had time to catalog every delicious whimper she made in the back of her throat. Each sharp inhale that pressed her breasts to his chest. Every caress of his fingertips along her narrow waist. The flicker of her tongue along his, her hands growing bolder as she stroked up his chest and over his shoulders. Her cinnamon-sugar flavor stirred his hunger, stoking the urgency building behind his zipper.

One more minute...

A warning bell clanged in the back of his head, alerting him that his "one more minute" had already gone on too long. With superhuman effort, he forced himself to loosen his grip on her waist. He levered back to look at her, breaking the kiss.

Her hazel eyes remained heavy-lidded, her focus unclear until she pulled her attention up to meet his gaze.

"What are you doing? Why did you stop?" Her pupils dilated, her tongue darting out to moisten her lips.

His heart hammered so loudly that the nature sounds vanished. The birds, the breeze, the rustle of small animals in the underbrush off the deck. Everything seemed silent except for the roar of his blood in his ears.

"I didn't want to pressure you if you weren't ready

for more." He dragged in deep breaths, willing his pulse back to normal. "About the bloodless thing…" He shook his head, disappointed with himself for needling her when she'd already been on the defensive. "You don't need to prove anything to me."

"No kidding. I'm pretty sure I have a stronger sense of self than that." Her hands began to slide away from his shoulders.

Ryder caught them, pinning them to his chest before she could take them back. "Wait a minute. If you're not proving a point, why are you kissing me?"

She stiffened. "Excuse me? *You* kissed *me*."

"I realize that. And I want to keep on kissing you. But not if you're going to fly back to the arms of some other guy tomorrow."

Her eyes narrowed a moment, scrutinizing him. He hadn't meant to reveal the dark jealousy for the man who wasn't yet her fiancé, hadn't even acknowledged that it lurked inside him until now.

Some of the tension eased from her at his admission while a breeze stirred a few dry leaves at their feet, rustling noisily. "I won't. You're right that I shouldn't accept someone as a partner just because they meet predetermined criteria. This week apart has made me reevaluate our relationship."

Relief whooshed through him at her reassurance. He hadn't realized how much he hated the idea of her marrying this guy until that moment. Since when was he so damned invested in her personal life?

She glanced at her feet, where a small whirlwind of fallen leaves danced around her white tennis shoes and his boots. When she looked up again, her eyes had a glimmer of a fire barely banked.

"Furthermore," she continued, her voice pitched low, "I told myself if I couldn't even picture his face when you were around, I had no business getting engaged to him."

Her words were a balm to his soul one minute. And the next, they lit him on fire. He nodded his satisfaction.

"That's why you kissed me."

Her breath huffed faster as her gaze dipped to his mouth. "I didn't see the point in denying something we both wanted."

His body steeled at the implication, his grip tightening where he held her hands in his.

"Hell no, there's no point." He drew her arms up, fastening them around his neck before he skimmed his palms along her body, gliding along her curves to land on her hips.

Tug them closer.

Her breath caught. Her lips still glistening from where he'd kissed her before. Desire squeezed his middle in a tight fist.

"We never purged this from our system when we were young," Jessamyn added, her fingers tangling in the ends of his hair, her body rocking closer. "Maybe now, if we indulge the attraction just this once, we can put it behind us and move on for good."

Just once?

He didn't agree with that statement based on the

hunger raging like an inferno inside him. Yet, for now, it was enough to know he could taste her again.

His body felt the pull of need radiating from her, and he was powerless to deny what she wanted. Especially when he'd dreamed about her every night this past week.

"We can indulge it all right," he muttered, lifting her higher against him so that he could kiss her without bending down. Her sweet curves dragged over him, scrambling his brain and making it imperative to have her underneath him. Or on top of him. Wrapped all around him. "I'll indulge your every last need for as long as you'll let me."

For a moment, their gazes collided. Locked.

"Yes. I want that." She cupped his jaw, her fingers stroking his cheekbone while their ragged breaths met and mingled.

He claimed her mouth the way he'd longed to in his car four days ago. The way he'd dreamed about ten years ago, before he'd let her chase her dreams.

Back then, he'd known they were both too young for anything permanent. He hadn't wanted to derail her dreams. And he knew he'd have to focus on his own goals as well. Now? She was all woman, and she knew what she wanted.

She kissed him like she'd been dreaming about this for as long as he had. Her tongue meeting and mating with his, her hips tilting toward him. The friction of her body made him forget everything but pleasing her. Providing what she needed.

Lifting her higher against him, he turned to bring

her indoors. With a sexy moan, she wrapped her legs around his waist, anchoring herself to him in a way that lined up the hard bulge in his jeans with the soft warmth between her thighs.

The pressure robbed him of every thought but being inside her, a need that seized him like a biological imperative he had to fulfill *now*.

"Jess," he growled her name like a warning as he opened the French doors into the wide-open space surrounded by windows. "If you keep that up, I'll never last."

"Really?" She broke the kiss just enough to say the word against his lips. "Are you suggesting I might have some power over your legendary self-control?"

Ah, damn.

She'd once accused *him* of being the bloodless one, back when he'd told her that a relationship would never work. That he'd only get in the way of her dreams.

But they weren't delving into that ancient history now. Not when she was wriggling against him like she couldn't wait to get her clothes off. Not when they were alone with a bed just a few more yards away.

"You've always had power over me." He let his hands roam over her hips until he palmed the rounded contour of her ass. Her shorts just barely covered her, his fingers grazing the tender flesh beneath those curves. "The difference is, now I'm not fighting it."

When his shins met the barrier of the mattress on

a low platform bed, Ryder dropped her onto the center of the fluffy white duvet. He backed away to work on the buttons of his shirt, his gaze never leaving her.

A sexy, speculative gleam was in her hazel eyes as she lifted her crop top tee up and over her breasts. White lace barely hid them from his view, and she wasted no time popping open the front clasp to slide off the bra, too.

His mouth dried right up at the sight of her dark pink nipples, her breasts swaying as she moved to the edge of the bed and stood up again.

He wasn't sure he remembered his own name by the time she hooked her thumbs in her jean shorts and wiggled them off her hips.

"That's a good thing," she purred as the denim slid down her thighs. "Because I'm not fighting it, either."

Four

For an instant, standing in front of Ryder in a pair of panties, Jessamyn flashed back to the last time she'd been this close to naked with him. The time she'd been ready to give him her virginity.

And he'd been too much of a gentleman to take it since he already knew they had no future together.

Ryder had shredded her heart and her pride all in one blow.

He wasn't backing out on her this time, though. She saw the fire in his eyes that told her he wanted this every bit as much as she did.

Just once, she promised herself. One time with Ryder and they would come full circle. She could move on. Excise him from her life without wondering about what they'd be like together.

Then his hands were moving, unfastening the rest of the buttons on his shirt while he toed off his boots. When he shrugged out of the shirt and moved to his jeans, Jessamyn's gaze locked on his torso, the road map of ridged muscle enticing her closer.

Closer.

As she reached to caress him, however, he imprisoned her wrist with one hand, spinning her around so that her back was pressed to him.

"Jess. Jess. I want you too much." He buried his face in her hair, his words warming her neck and her shoulder as he spoke. "Let me touch you first so I can make this last."

Releasing her wrist, his fingers drifted lower on her belly, sliding beneath her underwear.

Her head lolled back against his shoulder as pleasure and anticipation wound through her. "It doesn't matter," she protested, her breath coming in ragged puffs.

"It does to me. I need you to feel good." He scraped aside her hair with his free hand so that his lips were next to her ear. "Will you let me do that for you first?"

Her knees buckled a little as his fingers slid through her wetness, finding the pulsing center of her sex. A gasp raked up her throat at the feel of him there, circling the swollen flesh.

Over and over.

"Oh. Ryder," she managed brokenly, grateful when his other arm anchored her beneath her breasts. Securely held, she was able to remain upright while he sought out the touches that made her breath catch. "But I can't put my hands on you like this. It's not fair to you."

Her whole body spasmed as he reversed the path of his circling fingers, going backward. Fast and slow. Slow and fast. Building a fever inside her.

"You can't guess how much I want to touch you this way." His voice was pitched so low, so deep, it dragged her deeper under the seductive spell of what he was doing to her. "How much it cranks me higher seeing you like this."

She felt the pleasure tightening between her hips, knew she was close to flying apart.

"Yes. Yes, please," she murmured through the haze of desire. She couldn't stop her hips from grinding into his, taking the measure of the hard ridge pressed against her curves.

"I can't wait to watch you." The low insistence of his words made her head roll back and forth against his chest.

Then, the arm banding around her ribs shifted so that he palmed one breast. His thumb rubbed the nipple, mirroring the way he touched between her legs.

And just that quickly, she went hurtling over the edge, headlong into a fresh abyss of pleasure. Through every last convulsion, Ryder held her close, teasing more sensation from her body. She twisted against him, shamelessly seeking all that he had to give.

When she went still at last, heart slamming with

the overload, she pried her eyes open and lifted her head from his shoulder, feeling unsteady on her feet.

He must have known, because no sooner had she thought it than he lifted her in both arms and carried her to the bed.

This time she lay there trying to recover enough equilibrium to pay him back for the way he'd made her feel. Dragging in deep breaths while she watched Ryder through heavy-lidded eyes.

He shoved his jeans off his hips, taking his boxers and his socks before she'd even caught her breath.

And oh. Wow.

The sight of him made her inner muscles contract again, the empty ache intensifying.

"I have condoms," she offered, remembering the strip she'd put in her bag last winter. "I left my purse in your truck." She'd been changing them out seasonally for years even though she hadn't used one in longer than she could recall.

Was it any wonder that orgasm had felt so incredible?

And yet it hadn't been enough. She needed the deeper intimacy of him inside her. The completion of feeling him there.

"Housekeeping makes sure there are some in here," he assured her, reaching into the bedside drawer of a simple wooden nightstand. Retrieving a packet.

"Let me," she urged, taking the foil from him and ripping it open. "I want to touch you."

Kneeling up to the edge of the bed, she reached for

him. She stroked her fingers along the hot length of him while his breath hissed quietly between clenched teeth. He felt so good. She hated to cover him, imagining how it might be to have him without the layer between them. But what was she thinking?

Clumsily, she positioned the protection and rolled it into place, a thrill shooting through her at the gleam in his eyes.

A shudder trembled up her spine as his arms enveloped her, his body pressed to hers.

"Do you know how many times we've done this in my head?" he asked as he guided her down to the mattress. Covering her.

Her throat dried up. His question probed at her emotional defenses, stripping away more than just her clothes.

"More times than I should admit," he continued, not requiring an answer from her. His hands guided her hips where he wanted them, his steely hardness settling against her sex in a way that made stars flash behind her eyelids.

"Ryder," she murmured softly, desperate to lose herself in the physical and ignore the warmth of feeling in her chest. "Why aren't you inside me already?"

"Look at me," he commanded, stroking her hair away from her face. "I want your eyes on me when that happens."

When she did as he asked, their gazes connected, and his hips pushed forward.

She'd never been vocal in bed before, but a shout

built in her throat now, a hoarse cry of pleasure that broke free as he went deeper. Deeper.

Breathless, she gripped his shoulders tighter, her legs wrapping around his hips to accommodate more of him. All of him.

"Don't move," he rasped, his fingers sinking into her hips to keep her in place. "Need a minute. You feel too good, Jess."

Her teeth sank into her lip as she tried to hold still. In that moment, she felt his heart gallop faster while the rigid length inside her pulsed.

How could she *not* move?

"Um. Ryder?" Her breath whooshed in and out of her lungs, the vein beneath one eye ticking. She was hyperaware of every inch of her body. "The struggle is real for me, too."

He made a sound that might have been a laugh or maybe a cry of despair. Maybe a little of both. But whatever he was feeling, he seemed to give in to what they both wanted.

His hips began to move in a rhythm that made her forget everything else. Everything but this. Him.

All Jessamyn could do was hold on, letting the sensations build again, the anticipation pushing her higher. Her brain blanked of thoughts, her focus narrowing to Ryder. To the connection that had never gone away between them.

Even now, that bond threatened to take over. To eclipse everything else until it was the only thing she could see and feel.

Overwhelmed, she had no choice but to close her

eyes again, to focus on the physical part that was incredible enough without the complication of other feelings.

At the same time, Ryder slowed to reach between her thighs and massage the same spot that had given her an orgasm earlier. He grazed those places lightly at first, then picked up speed, using what he'd learned before to drive her closer to completion.

She wound her fingers in his hair, pulling too hard but unable to stop herself as he found exactly where she needed to be touched. Her feminine muscles seized, contracting over and over again in a way that must have touched off his release, because he went rigid above her a moment afterward.

His shout drowned out hers, the sound vibrating through his chest and hers, too, so that she felt it as much as she heard him. Helpless as wave after wave of release unwound, she bent her forehead to his shoulder, kissing him there. Biting gently while his body tensed and twisted through his own finish.

For long moments afterward, the only sounds were their harsh breaths and the pounding of their hearts. Hers slowed before his, but eventually, they both quieted. Ryder shifted away from her, withdrawing to dispose of the condom before falling back on the pillows next to her.

In the recesses of her brain, she knew she should probably make an excuse to leave. To resurrect the barriers that had crumbled between them this morning. But the residual effects of multiple partner-induced orgasms were too heady for her brain to pick her way through the potential land mines of that conversation.

Besides, the bed felt so comfortable, especially as Ryder flipped a quilt over her and stroked her hair from her face. She shouldn't like that so much when they couldn't be together again.

"I've been awake since three a.m. baking with Fleur," she reminded him as her eyes drifted closed. Really, she shouldn't feel this relaxed after sex with an old crush. Sex that couldn't be repeated when her stay in Catamount was very temporary, and Captain Earth would never leave his Colorado ranch. "I may close my eyes for just a second."

She would leave in a minute. Tell Ryder to take her home so she could resume her search for evidence to support her case against her father's will contest. Today was just a way to get Ryder out of her system for good. To have the closure he'd denied her ten years ago.

It would have been a hell of a lot easier to truly feel "closure" if the sex had been terrible. Especially when she feared she'd be craving a repeat of what had just happened between them and that would be unacceptable.

Luckily for her, self-discipline was Jessamyn Barclay's middle name. Because she had a mission in Catamount this summer, and it didn't have anything to do with Ryder Wakefield.

Jessamyn studied a map of Northwestern Colorado spread out on the picnic table in the backyard, two days after the toe-curling encounter with Ryder. Sun warmed her shoulders as she browsed Routt County for potential land deals—just out of curiosity, because real estate was her jam—hoping the break in her workday would take her mind off the man who loomed ever-present in her thoughts.

And it wasn't Brandon, even though her phone chimed again with a call from him. Her gaze went to her phone vibrating on the redwood table, knowing she needed to talk to him.

To tell him they couldn't go through with an engagement.

Steeling herself for the confrontation that she'd been delaying, she tipped her face up to the noonday sun and dragged in a deep breath. Then answered the call.

"Hey, B," she answered softly, the old shorthand for his name falling from her lips.

They'd met in the master's program at NYU, first as friendly rivals for top honors, later as study partners who motivated the best from one another. That dynamic had continued into their roles at Barclay Property Group, where she'd convinced her father to interview Brandon straight out of school. He was a strategist who was great with numbers. Jessamyn excelled on the client-facing side, calming high-strung investors, luring reluctant sellers into deals, and finding the elusive sweet spot that made everyone at the negotiation table happy.

She would hate to lose the synergy of their partnership. But she also couldn't afford to let him think this marriage could happen.

"Jessamyn, did you get the deal memo on the Cartwright sale?" he began without preamble, the sounds of a busy deli lunch counter echoing behind him. A bell ringing. Sandwich names shouted out over the dull rumble of a crowd. "The seller is back-pedaling about every aspect she agreed to last week."

"I did. And I was just about to call her." That wasn't strictly true, but she would do that next. For now, Jessamyn folded up the map on the picnic table and pushed it aside, reminding herself that her business was still in New York, not Catamount. "Can I talk to you about something else first? Once you have your food?"

She knew the deli close to the Barclay headquarters in Midtown Manhattan where he grabbed most of his lunches. Sometimes she joined him for a bite. In the summers, they'd walk to Bryant Park and sit outside.

"Sure thing. I'm on my way out the door now."

Her heart rate sped as she listened to the door chime as he exited. The traffic noise as he walked away from the building. This might not be the ideal time to tell him she didn't want to go through with the engagement scheme, but she'd delayed long enough.

"It's just that I've been thinking more about us as a couple long-term, and the more I consider it, the more I believe it will be a mistake." There. The truth was out.

In a nutshell, that was it.

Brandon didn't sound too pleased when he drew in a sharp breath, stifling a curse.

"Are you kidding me right now?" he asked, his voice sounding close on the phone as if he'd tucked the device under his chin. "When I've already been ring shopping and we've gone over the details twenty times, from the honeymoon in the Maldives to the home on Central Park South?"

Guilt stabbed through her.

They had talked about their plans in detail often enough. Perhaps that had been her way of putting off actually acting on them.

"I just don't think we should let my father dictate what happens with our romantic lives." Rising from the picnic table bench, she walked toward the goat pen where Gran's Nubians bleated and cavorted through the grass. "It seems sort of like…selling out. Like a cold approach to marriage."

She cringed as she heard herself use Ryder's words.

"Where is this coming from?" Brandon asked, his tone aggravated. Impatient. "Because this is straight out of left field for me, Jessamyn. We have talked this over at length."

"I realize that, and I'm sorry that I allowed my father's preferences to have such sway over me for so long." Because that's what it came down to. If not for the pressure from her dad, she would have never considered marrying Brandon in the first place. At best, they were friends with very occasional benefits. Hardly the foundation for a marriage.

Especially now that she'd known Ryder's touch and what real passion felt like.

The strangled sound Brandon made might have been another curse. Or a wry laugh.

"That's great you've figured that out. And thanks for letting me know on my lunch hour. Well done, Jessamyn. And since we're such experts in cold mergers, how about you make that phone call to the seller in the Cartwright deal now that you've given me the axe?" The fury in his voice surprised her.

She couldn't remember the last time she'd seen him truly angry. And never with her.

But she knew her timing hadn't been the best.

"You deserve better, Brandon," she said softly, reaching over the fence to pet the brown-and-white goat. "And I'll call the seller now."

She wasn't surprised when he disconnected the call without further comment.

And while one piece of her felt free from the weight of a connection that wasn't meant to be, another part of her echoed with the hollowness of a new realization.

Her father had almost talked her into an engagement she didn't want just because it would secure the legacy of his business.

How many other times had he steered Jessamyn into something that wasn't right for her, just because it was what he'd wanted?

A week after sharing the best sex of his life with Jessamyn, Ryder recognized that she was now officially avoiding him. He didn't like being ignored, and her flagrant evasion was wrecking his morning ride with his buddy.

Reining in his sorrel stallion, Flame, alongside his best friend, Drake Alexander, Ryder could see Jessamyn's retreating figure. The Alexander Ranch butted up against the Barclay family's Crooked Elm property, and Ryder had been hoping to see Jess today since she hadn't returned his texts. Ryder had driven her home after she'd fallen asleep beside him that morning. She'd seemed okay then. A little distant, perhaps, but he'd put that down to the awkwardness of sex outside a relationship. No doubt he'd been quiet, too, since he'd been processing what their mind-blowing encounter had meant.

But he'd told her he would call her after his next round of mountain rescue training with a crew of his SAR friends in Steamboat Springs. Yet when he'd returned to Catamount two days ago, she hadn't answered his call or texts.

Drake had asked him to review his winter rangelands where he was considering installing wind turbines, and they'd been riding back to the stables when Ryder had spotted her.

Drake nudged his paint mare, Pearl, toward the four-rail fence where Ryder had slowed to a walk. "Is that Jessamyn?" he asked, following Ryder's gaze where a slender figure vanished into the tree line near the creek.

"If it had been Fleur, I'm sure she wouldn't be walking away," Ryder observed dryly, wishing he felt as composed inside about Jess's defection as he forced himself to sound.

But the truth was, she'd dominated his thoughts all week, memories of their time together so vivid he couldn't stop replaying them.

"I thought you two were ancient history?" Drake slowed to a stop, then reached forward to pat Pearl on the neck.

Until that moment, Ryder hadn't even realized he'd come to a standstill himself. But he found himself straining to see beyond the ranch grasslands in the foreground to that thicket of juniper trees. To the Crooked Elm main house.

"We are." He needed to start believing that. Hadn't she told him their time together would be just once to get the attraction out of their systems?

He should be relieved, since he wasn't ready to come forward with the story about Mateo Barclay anyhow. Keeping what he knew about her father to himself now when the guy was contesting Jessamyn's inheritance was no easy task. It would simplify things for him to keep his distance while he kept an ear to the ground about the situation. He wouldn't share what he knew about Mateo unless absolutely necessary. And even then? He struggled mightily with the ethics of sharing something learned in a triage situation.

"And yet?" Drake prodded, swatting at a deerfly. "I sense more to this story."

"There may still be some chemistry," he admitted, unwilling to deny something that would surely be obvious to anyone who observed them together. And considering Drake wanted to marry Jessamyn's sister one day, chances were good he'd see the pair in each other's company.

If Jess ever stopped avoiding him.

Drake looked meaningfully toward where the middle Barclay sister had disappeared. "Chemistry or animosity?"

Ryder gave a rueful laugh as he tipped his head to remove his Stetson and fan himself with the brim. The late-July heat had picked up since they'd started their ride shortly after noon. The sun blazed hot now.

"Chemistry doesn't change who we are or what we want out of life. Jess is hell-bent on running her father's real estate business in New York and—" He stopped himself. Shook his head. "Well, can you picture me anywhere but in a saddle or on the side of a mountain?"

Drake gave a low whistle. "Did it really come down to that? You two were that serious?"

Ryder jammed his hat back into place, uncomfortable with the sharing. Normally, he didn't feel a need to unburden himself of personal stuff. It was indicative of how much Jessamyn had gotten under his skin that he was talking about any of this now.

"Like you said, ancient history." Ten years ago, he hadn't allowed his relationship with her to progress far enough for their differences to matter, since it wouldn't work between them anyway.

And about a year later he'd discovered something about her father that could turn her life upside down.

He knew he would never be able to hide something like that from a woman in his life. Even in the short time they'd been together since she'd returned for this visit, Ryder had felt the burden of it weighing him down. So why was her defection bugging him so much now?

"I'm sorry to hear it," Drake said finally, his brown eyes assessing. "I always liked all the Barclay women. It was a damn shame Antonia's son turned out to be such a jackass. That divorce did a number on his daughters."

Ryder hadn't been as close to the family as Drake had been when they were younger. He hadn't met Jessamyn until he'd been a teen working summers at a local rodeo, but then, Jess had never been a year-round resident. She'd shown up sporadically those last summers before she relocated to New York.

He was curious about Drake's impression of Mateo. Maybe his friend would have helpful insights.

"Hey, I was—"

Before he could get the rest of his thoughts out, a woman's scream cut through the quiet afternoon.

Five

"It's okay, puppy. It's okay," Jessamyn murmured to the agitated—massive—dog whose sudden growl from the woods startled a scream out of her.

She'd been hurrying along the creek to return to the house after spying Ryder on horseback with Drake Alexander on the neighboring property. A fierce growl from a thicket had scared her, and for a panicked moment, she'd thought a wolf had been eyeing her.

But a second look at the muddied and matted beast told her it was no threatening predator, but a Great Pyrenees caught in an illegal trap. Fury seized her even as a rush of sympathy for the frightened creature forced her closer to assess the situation and see if there was any hope of freeing it without endangering herself or the animal. She already had her phone in hand to call the state wildlife department for guidance when the ground beneath her feet vibrated with the sound of approaching horses.

And even though she'd been doing her best to avoid an awkward encounter with Ryder after what had happened between them, she'd never been so relieved to see someone. Ryder and Drake Alexander approached, a matched set of sleek horses, broad shoulders and Stetsons. Yet it was Ryder who commanded her full attention. Who sent her heart tripping in spite of her fear for the scared pet nearby.

"Jess? Are you okay?" Ryder's eyes were fixed on her as he secured a sorrel stallion to a tree and then made his way down the incline toward the water where she stood.

"I'm fine, but there's a dog in a foot trap down here." Her gaze flicked to the victim, whose head swung between her and the newcomers. His earlier growl had given way to anxious yelps, his rear paws dancing back and forth while his left front paw remained caught.

"Help is here," she assured the shaggy white canine while it followed her movements with liquid brown eyes, its ears pinned back. She kept her voice low. Soothing. "They'll know just what to do, I promise."

She didn't doubt their competence for a moment. Good ranchers understood animals, and they made it their business to treat them all with care and compassion.

The Great Pyrenees answered with a frustrated whine.

"Is he hurt?" Ryder called out as he reined in a couple of yards away. He was off his horse in no time, swearing at the sight of the trap. "Those are illegal. No way anyone got the special permit required to put that on your land."

Still keeping her distance, Jessamyn focused on the spot where the trap met the paw. The fur was dirty and wet and he kept shifting around, whimpering, as if he could free himself with enough movement. A fresh wave of empathy made her wonder how long he'd been out here scared and alone.

On the hill above them, Drake dismounted a moment behind his friend. "I'll get a log or something to put the trap on. They're easier to open if you have a hard surface to slide underneath it."

In the meantime, Jessamyn returned her focus to the ensnared pet.

"He's a little muddy, so it's hard to get a good look at the paw." She'd been careful to keep enough distance so as not to get bitten if the dog felt threatened. Only now, as Ryder neared, did she glance up at him again to see the rope in his hands. "What's that for?"

"We'll need a leash after we free him. It looks like he has tags, so someone will be glad to have him back home safely." Ryder reached her side, his palm finding the middle of her back. When their eyes met, his were full of worry. Concern. "That scream of yours scared the hell out of me."

Her mouth went dry at his expression. At the answering awareness of him.

The moment lasted only a second, and then he was all business, calling up the slope to his friend. "Drake, do you have anything we could use for a muzzle while we work on the trap?"

"Sure thing," Drake answered as he strode back toward his horse, a flat gray rock in one hand.

"You'll be able to extricate him?" Jessamyn asked, needing the reassurance. "I keep wondering how long he's been out here."

"I'll bet not more than a day from the looks of him." Ryder hung the length of coiled rope on a broken pine tree branch nearby. "But I've got a half sandwich in my saddlebag if you want to grab it for him while we disengage this big guy. The container it's in would make a good water dish if you bring that, too."

"I'm on it." She hurried up the hill, glad to have a task that would help.

She passed Drake on her way up. He carried a red bandanna now in addition to the flat gray rock. Some of her worry must have shown on her face, because Fleur's rancher boyfriend gave her shoulder a pat as he walked past.

"He'll be okay," Drake promised. "And we'll find whoever laid that trap."

She'd been so concerned for the dog she hadn't thought much about the legalities of the device yet. But how had it ended up on Crooked Elm land? Fleur would never set a trap, of course, and she was the

only one who had access to the property in the past
month.

Besides Josiah Cranston.

She stopped for a moment, remembering the tenant for the Crooked Elm rangelands. The guy was
a creep who had ignored the "vacate" order they'd
given him as soon as he'd discovered that Antonia
Barclay's will was being contested. He'd promptly
informed them that since they weren't legally recognized as the owners of the property, they couldn't
demand he leave.

Legally, he had a point. But Cranston had taken
advantage of their grandmother for years, using more
of the acreage for grazing than he was supposed to,
and getting the land at a cheap price by promising to
install an irrigation system, which had never materi-
alized. Could he be enough of a dirtbag to set traps
on the property, too? This particular acreage wasn't
even the part he paid to use.

Reaching into the saddlebag on Ryder's tall sorrel quarter horse, Jessamyn found the leftover lunch
and the plastic container, then hurried back down
the slippery incline strewn with pine needles and
dead leaves. Already, the dog had the red bandanna
tied around his snout to keep him from biting while
they helped him. Ryder stood over the furry captive,
keeping the big animal still between his knees while
Drake slid the rock under the trap.

Her heart caught in her throat at the sight of them,
taking so much care with the dog. Even as she moved
down to the creek's edge to fill the plastic container

with water, she kept one eye on Ryder's hands as he steadied the creature's shoulders and crooned words of comfort.

"…and you'll be clean and dry in no time," Ryder told the dog while Drake pressed on the sides of the trap with both hands. "You'll have a belly full of vittles and a healed-up war wound that all the lady dogs are going to swoon over."

Warmth curled through her at the gentle way he coaxed the frightened pup. Even when the trap opened around the injured paw, Ryder moved the limb out slowly and carefully, keeping the rest of the big animal still.

Jessamyn hastened over with the water as Drake tossed aside the trap. "Should I pour this on the cut to clean him up?"

At Ryder's nod, she washed away the mud and caked blood until they could see the wound beneath the snarled fur.

"We could use a wrap for that raw patch," Ryder observed. "The good news is it looks like an abrasion wound and not anything serious."

She saw a way to help. "We can use my sock to wrap him up. I wore knee-highs today in case there were ticks. One of these will be perfect." Her fingers moved to the laces on her tennis shoe.

Ryder petted the dog and continued to reassure the animal while Drake lifted the tag on his collar and observed, "His name is Phantom, by the way. And there's a phone number."

"Good." Ryder stretched a hand out for the coil of

rope he'd brought. "Looks like the link on his collar ought to be big enough to pass a line through."

Jessamyn noticed that the dog looked up at him, tail wagging slowly. Her heart melted a little.

Between the three of them, they got a makeshift bandage on Phantom's leg and the temporary leash secured to his collar. Carefully, they removed the muzzle once Phantom knew there was a meal in store for him in the form of the chicken sandwich. As the dog ate and drank from the refilled container, Drake contacted the owner and decided to meet at the closest nearby access road so Phantom wouldn't have far to walk. He seemed to bear weight without favoring his leg. Thank goodness he didn't need to be carried.

Jessamyn moved toward the discarded trap. Her anger returned, now that her fears for the dog had eased.

"We should bring this with us." She used a stick to lift the metal device. "No sense making it easy for an illegal trapper to reset it and use this again."

Ryder gave a grim nod as he took the contraption from her. "I'll call the wildlife department on the ride home."

Reminding her they'd be parting ways again. Soon.

She'd have to restart her mental clock on how many days she'd spent away from him. Somehow getting to seven had seemed like a feat after what they'd shared a week ago. Now she'd be back to zero and wondering how to put him out of her thoughts again.

From a few feet away, Drake moved to join them, settling his Stetson lower on his brow.

"Good news," he began, shoving his phone in his back pocket. "Phantom's owner is already on his way over here to pick him up. If I walk Phantom to the closest road, Jessamyn, would you consider riding Pearl to Crooked Elm? He'd be fine in the old pasture for a couple of hours until I meet Fleur for dinner tonight."

"Of course. I'd be happy to." She hadn't ridden since she'd returned to Catamount, but she'd been eager to be on horseback again. There'd been a time in her life when she'd ridden daily—during the school year at her family's home outside Dallas, and during the summers at Crooked Elm.

Decision made, she glanced up the hill at Drake's tall paint and prepared to take her leave of the men.

Until Ryder put a hand on the small of her back, steering her gently toward the mounts.

"I'm going with you," he announced, his tone grave. "If there's someone trapping on your land, Jess, we need to figure out who and why."

She could hardly argue with that. But for her own sanity—for the sake of getting through the next hour with Ryder at her side—she sure wished his touch didn't ignite a thrill she felt to her toes.

"You've been avoiding me."

Ryder hadn't seen a reason to mince words now that they were alone. He kept Flame to a walk as the horses picked their way along the creek toward

Crooked Elm. No sense hurrying back to the Barclay place when he had a few things to settle with the woman on horseback beside him.

His gaze roved over her long legs mostly bared by trim black shorts, especially now that she'd removed both her socks—one for Phantom, and the other she must have tucked away somewhere. She wore a long-sleeved white blouse that looked like it might be sun-protective, the fabric a nouveau kind used in hiking gear. No matter that he'd teased her about being a city girl, she had maintained her outdoors smarts. And her horsemanship, for that matter. She swayed in the saddle as easily as if she'd ridden daily for years.

She returned his gaze now, her expression defiant. "I don't see the point in spending time together when we both know things between us will never be anything more than what we already shared."

Irritation flared as he ducked a low-hanging branch. "Is that because you went back to your almost fiancé?"

He'd wondered about that more than once this week. Never before had he been a jealous person, but the idea of her still seeing the Manhattan big shot ticked him off no end.

"Of course not," she retorted immediately, frowning at him. "I might have allowed myself to get caught up in the idea of marriage for a time, but once I realized he wasn't the right one, I called and told him so."

The tightness in his chest relaxed, making him

too aware how much her answer had meant. "Then why do you think there will never be anything more between us?"

For a long moment, she didn't answer, the only sound the soft trudge of hooves over the pine-needle-strewn earth and the occasional twigs cracking underfoot.

"Honestly? I spent a long time being hurt by your rebuff ten years ago, Ryder." The stiffness of the admission underscored the truth of the words. "But eventually I did see your point. We want different things. Lead very different lives."

A rush of anger for his nineteen-year-old self surprised him with its force.

"Which were good reasons not to jump into a serious commitment. You were on the verge of a big future, Jess. I couldn't allow you to get sidetracked from your dreams."

"So you made the executive decision to end things with me rather than just say as much?" Her laugh was mirthless. "Not that it matters now, but I'd always prefer the truth to someone else figuring out what's best for me."

She'd meant the words to be biting. And yet Ryder knew she couldn't possibly realize how much they cut to the quick when he was keeping her father's secrets. The burden of that weighed still heavier as the main house came into view across a long, open pasture.

"All I'm saying is that we're not running the risk of falling in love anymore," he continued, readjusting the reins in his hands and steering Flame away from the creek bed to higher ground. "We're two consenting adults who happen to have a connection that nearly burned down the yurt when we were together. If you don't want any part of that—or me—again, then fine. No need to run for cover when we get within a mile of each other."

He'd never been much for casual relationships in the past, but Jessamyn Barclay wasn't just any woman. Whatever had happened between them a week ago had been special. Unique. Powerful. And he hadn't stopped thinking about her for more than ten minutes at a time this past week. He couldn't imagine not being with her again. Touching her. Tasting her.

Besides, the need to keep tabs on her father's court case hadn't gone away, and Jessamyn was his best hope of learning new developments.

"I've never run from a man in my life, Ryder Wakefield," she shot back, tossing her glossy hair behind her shoulder. "And I won't start with you. Now, don't you think we should call the wildlife department and focus on something more important, like who is setting illegal traps on my property?"

Conceding her point—even though he recognized very well that she was redirecting the topic on purpose—he withdrew his cell phone to report the incident as they neared the house. Drake had texted him a minute ago to let him know the Great Pyrenees belonged to the foreman on a neighboring ranch. The man had been overjoyed to be reunited with the dog—still technically a puppy despite his size—that had startled during a thunderstorm the day before and bolted out the front door.

Disconnecting his call as they reined in their mounts in the pasture area closest to the house, Ryder shared the response from the parks and wildlife department, which hadn't proven that encouraging. Although there were hefty fines for illegal trapping, finding the culprit often proved difficult.

"They suggested using a wireless wildlife camera." He dismounted as Jessamyn did the same. "Which is a good idea and I think I have one at the house that I can run out there later."

They ground-tied the horses while Ryder walked with her past a small shed and pen where three Nubian goats bleated noisily at them.

"Really? That would be great. If you don't mind." Something about the awkward cadence of the words, her rush to make sure it was no trouble for him, alerted him that she was still wary of getting close to him.

If he wanted to be with her again, he needed to proceed with caution.

"I want to." His own anger at the trapper added steel to his voice. "What kind of bastard traps illegally and on someone else's land to boot? You don't have any idea who would do that?"

He slowed his step as they reached the backyard, where a picnic table painted bright turquoise stood next to a birdbath surrounded by flowers in a riot of colors. Butterflies fluttered around the blooms, adding more rainbow shades to the mix.

Jessamyn lowered herself to the picnic table bench, facing away from the table to use the surface as a backrest. He took a spot by her on the bench, the old wood creaking quietly. Awareness tripped through him at her nearness, reminding him of the way they'd connected physically. Now that he had her attention again, he wasn't going to let her keep avoiding what happened between them. Sooner or later, they needed to confront it.

"I do have an idea, actually." She lifted her hair off her neck and twisted it in a complicated way that resulted in a low knot. "Or at least, I know that Josiah Cranston, my grandmother's tenant, has access to those lands. My sisters and I formally asked him to vacate when we thought we were going to clear probate and were preparing to sell the land."

He focused on what she said instead of thinking about how good her neck would taste. Or how much he ached to blow a cool stream of air to the heated place beneath her hair.

Instead, he forced his thoughts to what he knew of the disagreeable rancher—none of it good. His reputation for cheapness spilled over to his cattle, a failing that endeared him to no one. A man could cut corners with his equipment or maybe even the wages he paid his hired hands if times were really tough. But shortchanging livestock in your care?

There was no excuse for it.

"And he hasn't left?" A protective urge rose in him.

Jessamyn shook her head, crossing one leg over the other. "No. Legally, he doesn't have to until the ownership of the land is settled."

All the more reason to make sure the will was settled sooner rather than later. The knowledge of her father's shortcomings—his unworthiness to claim any part of Crooked Elm—ate at him. Made him all the more determined to find another way to help her since he hadn't shared what he knew with her.

"I can still talk to Cranston." He relished the opportunity to confront the guy, in fact. "And if he set that trap—"

"You don't need to get involved, Ryder. I appreciate the use of a camera if you have one, but Fleur and I will manage our business." She stood abruptly, the movement jolting the knot in her hair so the dark mass came tumbling around her shoulders. "Thanks for helping Phantom today."

As social cues went, she couldn't have sent him a more obvious one that she was ready for him to leave. More avoidance, damn it.

He rose to his feet, taking small comfort at the way her breath caught when he took a step closer. Just close enough to remind her how potent that connection was between them. He wouldn't push. But he wouldn't let her forget, either.

"No need to thank me. I went into search and rescue because I enjoy helping people." A smile pulled at his lips. "Dogs, too." He remained near her, breathing in her amber-and-vanilla scent, remembering the places he'd found that fragrance when he'd had her in his bed.

Behind her ears. At her wrists.

"I don't plan on requiring any more rescues this trip." She folded her arms as she squared herself to him.

Bold as you please, the same as she'd always been.

"Then I'll give you your space," he assured her. *For now*, he added silently to himself. But, unable to resist, he dropped his head to speak near her ear. "Just keep in mind I'm available for more than rescuing. Anytime at all."

He took it as a good sign that she made no smart comeback. No sharp retort. She swallowed visibly, her hazel eyes turning a darker green as she regarded him.

At least she'd be thinking about his offer.

Still, it didn't sit well to walk away from a woman he wanted so badly he could almost taste that amber-and-vanilla perfume on his tongue again.

Six

Jessamyn couldn't recall ever feeling so thoroughly turned on from a simple conversation with a man.

She forced herself not to watch Ryder Wakefield walk away from her after he'd practically handed her an engraved invitation back to his bed. An invitation that stirred memories she didn't want to have in her head right now when she needed all her focus on gathering evidence to fight her father's contest of Gran's will.

I'm available for more than rescuing. Anytime at all.

The echoing words sent a fresh shiver down her spine as she entered the cool interior of the Crooked Elm ranch house. The scent of cinnamon and sugar lingered around the clock with Fleur's newfound baking and catering businesses, and the incredible aromas enticed Jessamyn toward the bright yellow kitchen.

She couldn't have the no-strings affair that Ryder had tempted her with, so she would fill another hunger instead. Maybe if she gorged herself on sugar in the form of Fleur's one-of-a-kind pastries, Jessamyn would quit fantasizing about taking a big bite of a sexy rancher. Reaching for a plastic storage container on the counter sure to contain something tasty, Jessamyn started back at her sister's voice.

"Sooo…you and Ryder Wakefield?" Fleur stepped suddenly from the breakfast nook, a stoneware mug of coffee in one hand. She nodded toward the bay window behind the banquette. "I might have had a view of you two from my seat."

The youngest of the three Barclay sisters, Fleur bore little resemblance to Jessamyn or their older sibling, Lark. With copper-colored hair and gray eyes, Fleur had made smart use of her natural beauty and horsemanship skills to win rodeo pageants across five states after their father had cut her off financially. Jessamyn knew it hadn't been easy on Fleur to pay her own way through culinary school, but Fleur and Lark had both refused to make amends with their wealthy father for the sake of any support from him. For her part, Jessamyn had long blamed her mother for her role in the divorce that ignited stark family divisions. These past months since her grandmother's death were giving her reasons to rethink her dad's innocence, however.

For now, she was just grateful for the chance to salvage some kind of relationship with her sisters. Even though she was unaccustomed to anyone weighing in on her relationship decisions.

"Ryder and I are not…a thing," Jessamyn objected, while her body protested the news. "We're not anything."

She couldn't help that she wanted him. That was biology. A physical craving for intimacy didn't have anything to do with what was right or what made logical sense. Ryder had never shared her dreams or her vision for the future.

Although it had certainly come as news to her today that he'd broken things off with her ten years ago precisely because he understood that fact. All this time she'd thought he hadn't wanted her the way she'd hungered for him. The revelation that he'd given her up in spite of his own desires? That put a new spin on things.

She'd need to put that in perspective at some point. Figure out what it meant for them now, if anything.

Fleur's eyebrow lifted as she took a silent sip from her mug. Still clad in pajama pants and a pink sleep tee that said Less Talk, More Coffee, she leaned a hip against an archway separating the breakfast nook from the rest of the dining area. "Well, that clears up matters nicely."

Jessamyn opened the pastry container and helped herself to a *pain au chocolat* before closing it again.

"He was just helping me free a dog—"

Fleur held up her phone. "Drake told me all about it. I'm livid about a trap on our land."

"Me, too. Ryder said he might have a wildlife camera we could use to keep tabs on the area and see who comes to check the trap." Taking a bite of the croissant-like pastry, Jessamyn caught the crumbs in her free hand.

"My money is on Josiah Cranston." Fleur set aside her coffee mug on the Mexican-tiled countertop. "He made his displeasure clear when I gave him those lease termination papers."

"For all the good it did in getting rid of him," Jessamyn muttered darkly.

All three sisters were looking forward to the income the sale of the land would bring. At first, they'd also considered selling the ranch house, but now Fleur was making a pitch to keep it in their family. Her sister's sentimentality for the place had surprised Jessamyn at first, but spending time in Catamount again, remembering the warmth of their grandmother's house that hadn't been as tainted by their parents' unhappy split, she was beginning to see the appeal.

Well, beyond Fleur's love for Drake Alexander, of course. Jessamyn could also see the draw of Catamount. There was a strength and self-sufficiency to the people who lived in the foothills of the Rocky Mountains, a sense that they could fend for themselves no matter what came their way. Ten years ago, that hadn't meant anything to her when she had her eye on the prize of succeeding in her father's world.

But sometimes she wondered if she'd been seeking success for its own sake, or for her father's approval. She was so lost in her thoughts that it surprised her when Fleur called to her from the living room.

"Jess? You should see what I've been digging out this morning. Maybe it'll help us oust Cranston sooner rather than later."

Jessamyn took another bite of the chocolate pastry before setting it on a napkin for later. She brushed her hands over the sink to remove the crumbs before following her sister's voice into the whitewashed living area. With dark wooden beams overhead and the fireplace wrapped in tile, the room had all the Spanish Colonial touches that Antonia Barclay had loved. The dark wooden floor was partially covered with a worn cream-colored carpet while oversize leather chairs alternated with white sofas around the hearth.

But today, there were also boxes everywhere. Some open, some still closed, they were stacked on the coffee table and floor. A few spilled out their contents of papers and books onto the surrounding furniture.

A low whistle escaped her as she took it in. "What's all this?"

Curious, she walked over to one of the storage bins marked "Photos, hacienda rehab" to see what was inside.

"Gran's things from in the attic," Fleur explained, dropping to sit in one of the big leather armchairs. "I started pulling down boxes so we could search for documents that might support our claim that Gran wanted the property to go to us."

"This is excellent." Surprised at her sister's initiative, she glanced from the stack of old pictures to Fleur's determined face. All week while Jessamyn worked remotely, Fleur had been busy with catering jobs and baking, giving Jessamyn the impression that she wouldn't be much help with the court case. But clearly, Fleur had made time. "I didn't know Gran kept so much."

She picked up a handful of photos of the Crooked Elm in the days before Antonia had gone to work on the interior. Her and their grandfather smiling around a tall Christmas tree. Antonia in an apron, covered in flour as she worked in the old, tiny kitchen.

"Me, either. But I went in the attic because I wondered if there was any way to convert the space into a cathedral ceiling in the great room." In her quest to keep the ranch house, Fleur had been considering ways to make space for her own restaurant on the property—either in a separate building, or in an addition to the home. "And I found all this stuff tucked under one of the eaves in a crawl space."

"All we need to do now is go through it." Jessamyn guessed it could take days. Especially if some of the documents were written in Spanish, her grandmother's native language.

Jessamyn wasn't working a full schedule for Barclay Property Group while she was in Catamount, but she'd been juggling at least thirty hours a week since arriving. Now, she'd have to whittle that back

a bit to make time for the hunt for supporting documentation of Antonia's will. Her father wouldn't
be happy about that, but then, it was because of his
court case that she needed to do this.

As for Brandon… He wouldn't be pleased to lose
more of her time, especially on conference calls with
potential new clients when she was their most effi-
cient closer. In fact, she guessed he'd be more disappointed about a potential loss of business that her
absence might mean than he'd been about losing her
as a potential life partner.

"I've actually got a lot of catering commitments
in the next few days, but I have some time free next
week," Fleur said.

Jessamyn sank down to sit on the arm of one of
the sofas as she reached into a box and pulled out a
small book covered in dark leather. She swallowed
a sigh, unwilling to discourage Fleur, but frustrated
not to be making more headway with finding evidence. She really wanted to unearth something de-
cisive that would show their dad he couldn't win his
own way in everything.

As fun as it was to find old photos, she doubted
the ones in her hand would help.

"Sounds good. I'll get a head start this week and
we can finish together when you're available." An
idea had been circling around her brain ever since
she'd learned they'd need witnesses or written evidence to support their case. "You don't suppose Mom

would have anything in her possession that would support our claim? Old letters from Dad or Gran?"

Fleur glanced up from the diary, wariness scrawled in every delicate feature. "You're not seriously suggesting I ask Mom about letters Dad sent her?"

"Right. No sense walking over a potential land mine." She set aside the old square photos she'd been holding. "It took *us* almost a decade to start speaking again. It would probably take Mom that long to think about Dad without getting angry."

She ran a finger over a cut on her hand that she must have gotten while helping free Phantom. She wished the unseen cuts her family—and Ryder— had left on her would fade as easily as this small scrape would.

"And vice versa," Fleur reminded her shortly. A little sharply. "Not only is Dad no help to us, but he's the one actively gunning for our inheritance when he knows perfectly well Gran wanted us to have Crooked Elm."

Jessamyn tensed, bristling out of old habit. But her sister had a point and it was past time to acknowledge it. "Do you know why I took Dad's side? To start with, at least?"

She hadn't planned to share this with Fleur, but then, nothing about this trip was going the way she'd anticipated—from sleeping with Ryder and ending her engagement, to finding more to love about Catamount and her family.

Her father had been pressuring her to come back

to work, to give Brandon another chance, to focus on new clients. He was great at talking but not so good at listening. He needed Jessamyn at his side to persuade their clients that they understood what the clients wanted in their new property. She had the touch—personal and professional.

From the emails, texts and voice mails she was getting, Mateo was growing annoyed that she was deviating from his wishes. And Jessamyn was growing more frustrated at being on the outs with her father. Even Brandon was wondering if they should try again.

Jessamyn had to keep things under control both in New York and Colorado.

Fleur's answer came quickly as she flipped through the small volume in her hands. "Because Dad's ambitious, like you. Because you wanted to live the kind of life he was building for himself in New York instead of the slow-lane pace we lived in Texas."

"Later, maybe, those things mattered to me. But at first, during that initial awful year when Mom found out Dad cheated and she hated him so much—that didn't have anything to do with it." For a moment, the old hurt stole over her, so sharp she had to close her eyes for a moment and breathe through it.

When she opened her eyes again, Fleur stared at her curiously.

"Why, then?" Fleur ran her fingers over the cover of the leather book, then clutched it closer to her chest as she listened.

"Because she told me I was just like him." Not just once or twice. Over and over. Quickly swallowing the catch in her voice, she cleared her throat impatiently. "When I asked her to come to school for things—for myself, yes, but also in the hope of giving her something to think about besides her unhappiness with Dad—she told me I was being selfish. That I shared that in common with our father. That every time she looked at me, all she saw was him—the driven overachiever. She made me feel all the resentment she had for him. Every time I laughed or had a friend over or did well in school, she brought up how much we were alike."

And it had been no secret what Jennifer Barclay thought of her husband by then. Jessamyn had felt the pain of the words singed into her skin like a brand, along with all the ways it implied her own mother's dislike of *her*. Jessamyn had taken up her father's banner then and there, knowing she wouldn't be welcome on her mom's side.

How many life decisions had she made as a result of supporting her dad? Her career? Where she lived? She wanted to believe she'd chosen her path based on her passions and her skill set. But being back in Catamount was reminding her of other things she'd once enjoyed.

"She was battling depression, Jess," Fleur reminded her quietly.

Empathy registered along with regret for all the time she'd lost with her mother. But it hadn't been all bad. Her dad had put on a good face and shown up for her, whether it was chaperoning a Model UN field trip or driving her to dance competitions.

Although, looking back on it, had he fanned the flames of the division between mother and daughter?

"I know that *now*. But I didn't understand anything about what she was going through when I was twelve years old. Then, by the time I was old enough to realize what she'd been experiencing, we were already on opposite sides of the family battle."

The hurt and fallout of that time—learning that she'd abandoned her mom when her mother had been fighting for her health—had led Jessamyn to fall for the first man who'd treated her with kindness and understanding when she was eighteen. She'd been swept off her feet by Ryder's empathy and generous spirit, so different from the way her family members all guarded themselves. Then, when Ryder had abandoned her, too, she'd had zero emotional resources for shoring herself up afterward.

"Maybe *you* should ask Mom if she has anything to support our claim," Fleur suggested a moment later as she slid the leather-bound volume back into the closest box.

"Me? The Barclay daughter who has no relationship with her?" She shook her head, not understanding.

"It could be a way to start a dialogue with her again." Fleur held a hand up before Jessamyn could argue. "Just think about it. I'm convinced Gran left us Crooked Elm to help us find our way back together as sisters. Maybe it will help us heal some of the other stuff, too."

Like her broken relationship with her mother? Jessamyn seriously doubted that. Or maybe she was simply afraid to hope.

"First, I'm going to go through the boxes," she said instead, unwilling to disappoint her sister when Fleur had gone to the effort of bringing down all the papers from the attic. "Maybe talking to Mom won't even be necessary."

Fleur made no answer, but then, she didn't have to. Jessamyn recognized she was hiding from confrontation with their mother the same way she'd avoided Ryder all week. But her coping mechanisms had gotten her this far in life, and she was doing just fine so far, thank you very much.

Although, as a memory of Ryder's parting words—*I'm available for more than rescuing. Anytime at all*—floated through her head again, Jessamyn wondered if she'd be able to continue her avoidance strategy where he was concerned. For one thing, she was curious about his revelation today that he'd only broken things off with her ten years ago because he'd understood she needed to follow her dreams. She wanted to ask him more about that, but how could she without seeming like she just wanted another chance to tear his clothes off again?

Until she figured that out, she suspected she would need a whole lot more *pain au chocolat* to assuage the hunger still tingling through her even now.

* * *

Have you spotted any activity on the wildlife camera yet?

Ryder read Jessamyn's text after he got out of the shower, his wet hair dripping onto the screen since he hadn't been able to wait to dry off to read it.

Respecting Jessamyn's space proved a whole lot tougher than he'd thought it would be, but then, he'd known she was a strong-willed and fiercely independent woman. She wouldn't simply fall into his bed all summer long simply because they had amazing chemistry. If anything, the strong connection had probably rattled her into keeping her distance over the two weeks since they'd rescued the dog together.

Sure, she'd helped him install the wildlife camera so they could see if anyone came to check the trap, but she hadn't indicated she wanted to see him again. And how could he press her when he'd promised to give her some breathing room? But in the ten days since they'd installed the camera, she'd gotten in the habit of texting him in the evenings to ask about the feed that was still hooked up to his personal account and easier for him to check.

Which was why he hadn't been able to wait to dry off when he'd heard the notification chime at 10 p.m. The sound had a Pavlov's-dog type of effect on him, his body going on high alert at just the thought of an interaction with her. Because sooner or later, she would want to find out if their first time together had been a fluke. He couldn't believe he was the only one reliving those hours they'd spent in his bed.

Just showered, he typed back, taking a small amount of pleasure in putting that image into her head. Will fire up laptop in a sec and get back to you.

He could check the feed from the phone, but he was already signed in and had the page loaded on the other device.

Besides, he might have agreed to give her space, but he hadn't made any promises about the nature of their conversational topics. He didn't mind pressing a few of her buttons if it would speed her in his direction. Hell, he didn't mind pressing anything of Jessamyn Barclay's.

Maybe that was why he found himself typing again as he secured the towel around his waist and looped another around his shoulders before he walked out of the bathroom into the master suite.

I told you what I'm wearing. Or not. Care to repay me with a visual on you? He hit Send, not giving himself time to second-guess the message. If she thought for a second that he didn't think of her often, he wanted to disabuse her of the notion.

I'm covered in dust bunnies thanks to crawling in the attic. Still searching for supporting documentation of Gran's wishes.

Ouch. He felt the pang of guilt about the information he was withholding as he dropped onto the gray leather couch across from the fireplace in his suite. He used the towel around his neck to mop off his face and chest before pulling open his laptop on the coffee table.

Lucky dust bunnies. He input the words on his phone while his laptop fired to life. But sorry to hear you haven't found evidence yet.

He was certain it had to be out there. Because Antonia Barclay had definitely not wanted to give Crooked Elm to her son. Even Mateo Barclay knew that, whether or not he would admit it.

For a long moment, his phone remained silent and he wondered if Jessamyn was discouraged. He hated the thought of her wasting time looking through old papers to no avail.

I hope so, she typed finally. And something about those three lone words assured him he hadn't lost her. The connection between them was still there, and not just the on-screen kind.

Tapping the buttons on his laptop that would show him the last day's worth of camera footage in fast-forward mode, Ryder then turned his attention back to his phone. His hands might be tied as far as keeping the old confidentiality he owed her father, but Ryder could still give her a hint of where to look for answers without compromising any ethics, couldn't he?

I know you don't want to contact your mother about this, but what about one of your dad's girl-friends? he suggested, knowing which one would be ready to throw Mateo under the bus. Remember the one he was dating when you and I were together?

He told himself that wasn't pushing it. That he wasn't angling for Jessamyn to come over and see him in person for answers. With one eye on the camera footage, he was thinking about how much he wanted to see her again when his phone rang.

Caller ID showed his SAR commander.

Crap.

Stabbing the connect button, he already knew what the guy wanted. It was the only reason his SAR contact ever phoned him personally, let alone at this hour.

"Wakefield here," he answered at the same time he typed a final message of the evening to Jessamyn.

Will look at footage later, Jess. SAR duty calls.

Hitting Send, Ryder rose to dress for work. Normally, a search and rescue assignment consumed all his attention. But even after he hit the road five minutes later, his gear already in the back of his truck, Ryder couldn't shake the image of Jessamyn alone and frustrated at Crooked Elm, needing help he couldn't give her.

One way or another, when he got back he would think of a way to ensure she found the information she needed.

Seven

Blinking from the sunlight splashing over her face, Jessamyn awoke slowly from the deepest, thickest sleep of her life. Her head felt heavy. So did her limbs. What time must it be for her old bedroom at the Crooked Elm to be this bright? Birds trilled outside her window.

She never slept late.

"Jess? Can I come in?" Her sister's voice sounded outside her door.

"Of course you can," she answered, trying to sound alert since it seemed inexcusably lazy—for her, at least—to have just opened her eyes at…she lifted her cell phone to see the time…nine in the morning?

Fleur pushed the door to the small bedroom at the same time Jessamyn scrambled to a sitting position.

And while Jessamyn felt sloppy in her nightclothes, Fleur wore cute denim cutoffs and a cream-colored retro blouse with crocheted squares across the bodice and gauzy sleeves.

"Sorry to bother you." Fleur stopped short at the sight of her sister still in a black tank top and pajama shorts. "I didn't mean to disturb you, but I thought you'd want to know—"

"You didn't disturb me," Jessamyn protested, still feeling "off" somehow. Not tired. Not sick. Just like she was moving through peanut butter or something. "I'm usually up for hours by now. I guess I had trouble falling asleep last night or something."

All at once, she recalled Ryder's final text to her about going out on a search and rescue assignment. She gripped her phone tighter, seized with the need to follow up on his message. Make sure he was okay.

"It's fine. I assumed the early mornings you've put in helping me bake for the Cowboy Kitchen finally caught up with you." Fleur lowered herself to sit at the foot of Jessamyn's bed, tucking her bare feet under the white dust ruffle, a decorating leftover from Jessamyn's childhood. "And I hated to disturb you now, but I thought you should know that Ryder is out on a potentially dangerous search and rescue call."

Everything inside her went still.

"What do you mean? How do you know?" Straightening her spine, Jessamyn narrowed her focus to her sister. "Who told you that?"

"Everyone in the diner was talking about it this

morning. A couple of climbers got caught in a summer avalanche out in the Flat Tops Wilderness—"

"Avalanche?" Her heartbeat went into overdrive as her brain stumbled on the idea, cold fear wrapping itself around her throat. "How could that be? It's been seventy degrees out this week."

"A wet avalanche, according to everyone at the Cowboy Kitchen." Fleur scooted closer on the bed, laying a hand on Jessamyn's bare arm. "The snow on the peaks melts and makes the underlayer unstable."

"And Ryder is still out there?" Jessamyn swung her legs out of the covers, unable to sit still. "It's been almost eleven hours since he got the call. He texted me last night, and—"

Remembering their message thread, she turned on her phone's screen to see if there was anything else from him. But the last text she'd received from him had been about 10:45 p.m.

Worry sank in her gut like a stone. She opened a heavy chest of drawers near the bed and pulled out a fresh T-shirt and a pair of sweatpants.

"What are you doing?" Fleur asked, coming to her feet.

"I need to find out what's happening." The lethargy she'd felt on waking was gone, evaporating under the hot weight of regret that she hadn't followed up on Ryder's mission before going to bed. "Do you know where they are?"

"Somewhere near Pagoda Peak, I think. But you can't go out there, Jessamyn. They'll never let you near a rescue operation—"

"I know." Nodding, she pulled the sweatpants over her sleep shorts and then shimmied out of the tank top to yank the T-shirt over her head. "I was just curious. I could learn more at the diner, maybe. Or Ryder's house."

Jessamyn headed for the small Jack-and-Jill bathroom shared with the bedroom that used to belong to Lark. While Jessamyn ran her toothbrush over her teeth, Fleur smoothed the covers on the bed Jessamyn had left so hastily.

Fleur didn't ask her why she was so worried. But then, if her sister had known to wake her up with this news in the first place, obviously Fleur had a clue that Jessamyn's feelings for Ryder were more than just friendly.

So much for keeping him at a distance.

She just needed him to be okay.

"Do you want Drake to drive you anywhere?" Fleur asked, following her out of the bedroom and down the stairs. "He's worried, too."

The knowledge that Ryder's closest friend was scared as well didn't do anything to lessen her anxiety.

"There's no need." Grabbing the car keys for the rental she'd finally managed to obtain the week before, Jessamyn stuffed her phone in the pocket of her sweats and headed toward the door. "I'll be fine."

She just prayed that Ryder would be, too.

Because of their history, she told herself. Because he'd been her first love, and he was a good person. Her fears were rooted in that old bond and didn't have anything to do with what had happened between them a few weeks ago.

A sudden bout of queasiness stopped her as she put her hand on the doorknob. A wave of nausea forced her to stand still for a moment. Collect herself.

Backtracking to the fridge, Jessamyn grabbed a water bottle for the road. She'd be fine.

He'd be fine, too.

She was just being sentimental. Sensitive. The trip to Catamount was pulling all kinds of surprising emotions out of her—feeling nostalgia for a sense of family she hadn't experienced in too many years. Remembering how much she'd once loved this place. And, of course, memories of Ryder were tied up in all that.

Once she saw Ryder was okay, she would return to working on the case she was building against her father's claim on Crooked Elm. Then her life would return to normal.

Bone-weary, Ryder breathed a sigh of relief as he steered his work truck onto the private drive for Wakefield Ranch. The search for the missing climbers had taken half the night, and the rescue operation the whole morning, both parts hampered by miserable conditions. Leaving him wet, exhausted and scraped up from scrambling around rocky terrain in the dark. He'd showered and grabbed a couple of slices of pizza at the local firehouse where his team had convened afterward, but the damp cold from the slush on the mountain hadn't left him yet.

They'd found the climbers—alive—and brought them home successfully. Any other day, that would be enough to soothe the physical toll of rescue work. But today's assignment reminded him too much of another one. That first, long-ago SAR mission where Mateo Barclay had called for help to save his girlfriend who'd fallen down a ravine in an avalanche.

A fall she'd taken because of Barclay's negligence.

Squinting gritty eyes against the bright afternoon sun, Ryder scrubbed a hand over his chest, where a thorny ache of regret had lodged a decade ago. He would have mulled it over more, except that as the main house came into view, so did an unfamiliar sedan. And a very familiar feminine silhouette.

Jess.

His exhaustion faded, replaced by a new urgency to wrap her in his arms. The adrenaline rush that came from his work on the mountain could leave him buzzing for hours afterward, and he felt that surge to life again, igniting a hunger no other woman but this one could fill.

What was she doing here? The need to find out had him slamming his vehicle into Park the second he braked to a stop. Throwing the door open, he stepped down to the stone drive that curved in front of the entryway while his gaze hungrily tracked her movement toward him.

"Is everything okay?" he asked, closing the distance between them. He couldn't ignore the instinct to touch her, not when her hazel eyes locked on his, worry etched in her features. When he opened his arms, she flew into them. "What's wrong?"

Her soft curves molded to his body, the amber-and-vanilla scent of her skin and hair filling his nostrils. She felt so good. So right. Memories of their night together stole through his brain, fanning the flame of his hunger for her.

She tucked her head into his chest, her cheek pressed to a place just above his heart, her whole body tense. "I've been worried about you. I heard about the avalanche." For two heartbeats, she took deep breaths and seemed to steady herself before peering up at him again. "The local news was giving updates about the climbers, but they didn't say anything about the rescue workers."

Touched by her concern, he wanted to believe her fears for him meant something—emotions she'd refused to show him before now. Then again, how much worse would he feel about keeping secrets from her if their physical intimacy spiraled into something deeper?

He told himself to let her go. Relinquish the hold he had on her before they wound up right back in his bed. With an effort he edged away from her a step, just enough to insert an inch of space between their bodies. His hands remained fixed on her waist, though, his fingers not quite cooperating with the plan.

"I'm sorry you were worried. It was a long night because conditions went to crap. Too windy for the chopper to find the climbers, and too risky for the search dogs." He felt her sharp intake of breath at his words, saw the fear return to her eyes, and he quickly amended his decision to share the particulars. "But we found them. We all stayed safe, and we got them out of there without taking unnecessary chances."

By slow degrees, he felt the tension in her body relax.

"Thank God. That must have been scary." She exhaled a long breath but didn't move her hands from where they'd rested on his sides. Only now, as her anxiety seemed to lessen, did he allow himself to take in the sight of her. She'd obviously dressed hurriedly in a pair of sweats with a slightly rumpled white tee, her glossy brown hair tied in a crooked ponytail. She looked a far cry from the sleekly elegant executive he'd picked up at the airport a few weeks ago.

And damn, but he liked this side of her even more. It reminded him of the woman he'd fallen for ten years ago. The Jessamyn she'd been before she embraced a different life in New York. Dangerous thoughts when he needed to let her go.

The adrenaline still hummed inside him, needing an outlet.

"I should get in the house." He wrenched his hands away from her, a new kind of tension filling him now that hers had eased.

He took a step back, putting more space between them so her hands fell away from him. Regret for the loss of her touch crowded his insides, his body howling over the abrupt parting.

Jessamyn's forehead knitted in confusion. "I don't understand. Was it wrong of me to wait for you?"

"No," he told her vehemently in a voice too loud. Then, modulating his tone, he swallowed before he continued. "I'm flattered. I'm just—"

"Flattered?" She bristled, her shoulders straightening as she drew herself up to her full height. "Like I'm some kind of groupie?"

"That's not it," he assured her, his skin feeling too tight as he tried to recalibrate his response. But thoughts and reason failed him when all the heightened fears from the mountain—decisions he'd had to make in life-and-death situations—left him with no resources to navigate a dicey conversation.

And all the while, his brain taunted him with images of losing himself in Jessamyn's soft, giving body. Sweat popped along his shoulders as his boot heel hit a stone step. He hadn't even realized he was still backing away.

Jessamyn lifted her arms in surrender. "By all means, I'll let you get back to whatever it is you need to do. Sorry my worry delayed you—"

He stepped forward and caught whatever she'd been about to say with his mouth, sealing his lips to hers in the heated kiss he'd needed since the moment he stepped out of his truck. Knowing he didn't have the eloquence to argue right now, he just wanted this kiss to speak for him. He'd step away any second now. As soon as she got the message that he wasn't being selfish by retreating.

He was being respectful, damn it.

Except there was a chance that message was going to get lost if he continued to devour her like a starving man.

Breaking the kiss was one of the toughest things he'd ever done. But he would not take advantage of a vulnerable moment when Jessamyn had been worried about him. As he held her gaze in the aftermath of the explosive kiss, he hoped like hell his eyes did a better job of explaining that he was on edge right now.

That he needed her too much for finesse.

For a protracted moment, she stared up at him, her rapid breath huffing over his lips as she seemed to weigh what had just happened. Would she storm away, indignant that he'd kissed her into silence?

Or would some tender regard for him see beyond his knee-jerk reaction to the knot of emotions behind it? Perhaps she'd kiss him on the cheek and walk away again, return to avoiding him the way she'd done as much as possible over the past weeks. An idea that left him hollow as hell.

Ryder swallowed the lump in his throat, bracing himself for either one.

Instead, he watched as Jessamyn's hazel eyes shifted a shade greener. Brighter. The pupils dilated, the black center crowding away the mossy ring around the outside. A switch flipped inside him, his heart slugging heavy against his rib cage. His body understood that signal from her faster than his head could comprehend it. Everything inside him tightened. Tensed.

Turned hard as steel.

At the same moment, Jessamyn stepped closer to him, her gaze never breaking. With slow, deliberate movements, she laid her palms on his chest and smoothed them up and over his shoulders, leaving rippling sensations in their wake. Her hips tilted toward his, the contact eliciting a groan of pleasure from both of them.

"Take me inside with you, Ryder. Now."

Gratified by Ryder's instant response to her request, Jessamyn found herself almost running to keep up with his long strides up the covered walkway to his massive stone-and-log home. His grip on her hand was tight. Sure.

As if he had no intention of letting her go.

A shiver of anticipation tripped through her while he jabbed impatient fingers over the security keypad near the front door. The testosterone practically steamed off him in his jeans and work boots, a navy blue T-shirt bearing the logo for Routt County Search and Rescue stretched across his shoulders.

She hadn't come here for the purpose of mind-blowing sex. She'd been scared and emotional—two moods she had little experience dealing with. And maybe after the hours of fear, she was recognizing some of that adrenaline crash that seemed to take hold of Ryder now that his mission had been accomplished.

No way would she turn her back on him—on *this*—now.

Get ready to relax and indulge with your FREE BOOKS and more!

Claim up to FOUR NEW BOOKS & TWO MYSTERY GIFTS – absolutely FREE!

Dear Reader,

We both know life can be difficult at times. That's why it's important to treat yourself so you can relax and recharge once in a while.

And I'd like to help you do this by sending you this amazing offer of up to FOUR brand new full length FREE BOOKS that WE pay for.

This is everything I have ready to send to you right now:

Try **Harlequin® Desire** books featuring the worlds of the American elite with juicy plot twists, delicious sensuality and intriguing scandal.

Try **Harlequin Presents® Larger-Print** books featuring the glamorous lives of royals and billionaires in a world of exotic locations, where passion knows no bounds.

Or **TRY BOTH!**

All we ask in return is that you answer 4 simple questions on the attached Treat Yourself survey. You'll get **Two Free Books** and **Two Mystery Gifts** from each series you try, *altogether worth over $20*! Who could pass up a deal like that?

Sincerely,

Pam Powers

Harlequin Reader Service

Treat Yourself to Free Books and Free Gifts.

Answer 4 fun questions and get rewarded.

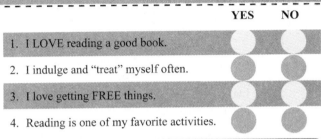

**We love to connect with our readers!
Please tell us a little about you...**

	YES	NO
1. I LOVE reading a good book.	○	○
2. I indulge and "treat" myself often.	○	○
3. I love getting FREE things.	○	○
4. Reading is one of my favorite activities.	○	○

TREAT YOURSELF • Pick your 2 Free Books...

Yes! Please send me my Free Books from each series I select and Free Mystery Gifts. I understand that I am under no obligation to buy anything, as explained on the back of this card.

Which do you prefer?

❏ **Harlequin Desire®** 225/326 HDL GRAN
❏ **Harlequin Presents®** Larger-Print 176/376 HDL GRAN
❏ **Try Both** 225/326 & 176/376 HDL GRAY

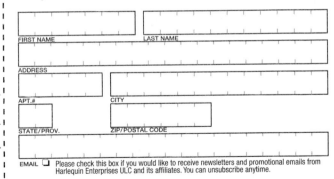

FIRST NAME   LAST NAME

ADDRESS

APT.#   CITY

STATE/PROV.   ZIP/POSTAL CODE

EMAIL ❏   Please check this box if you would like to receive newsletters and promotional emails from Harlequin Enterprises ULC and its affiliates. You can unsubscribe anytime.

HD/HP-520-TY22

HARLEQUIN Reader Service — **Here's how it works:**

"This way." He directed her through a huge foyer where glowing wood floors and high cathedral ceilings framed a small water feature in one wall, the sound of flowing water a musical greeting.

But she didn't have time to take in much beyond the split-log stairs leading up to the second-floor gallery. Ryder still gripped one of her hands tightly while she allowed the other palm to skim along the polished log handrail where elk antlers served as spindles. The scent of pine and cedar mingled in the air as she followed Ryder into the primary suite at the top of the stairs. Two patio doors opened onto a private deck from here, overlooking the green backyard, where gravel paths connected the natural stone pool area to the firepits and dining area.

Flip-flops smacked the wide plank floors as she wandered into the living area of the suite, her heart still racing. The sound of her shoes reminded her how little attention she'd paid to her appearance in the race to find out if Ryder was okay. A residual quiver of worry forced her to look at him now as he closed the door behind them, sealing them into the privacy of his bedroom.

Her throat went dry as she feasted her eyes on the ropes of muscle in his arms, the chiseled perfection of his pectorals that looked hewn from stone through his fitted cotton T-shirt. Memories of what he looked like without it put her feet in motion to meet him halfway across the room, her fingers itching to undress him.

"You're going the wrong way," he chastised her gently when she reached him.

His big palms settled on her hips as he steered her backward, deeper into the room. His thumbs strayed below the waist of her sweatpants, coming to rest in the hollow below her hip bones. Desire pooled low in her belly.

"Don't you want me walking *toward* you?" She couldn't keep her hands off him, her touch skimming up his arms to slide beneath the fabric of his sleeves.

"First and foremost, I want you in my bed." His voice was all gravel, low and rough. "Once you're there, I'll come to you."

A soft whimper escaped her, and she wondered at the plaintive sound that she'd never made before with a man. Normally, she took what she wanted in bed, comfortable with asking for what she needed. But this heady urge to give? And to feel so worked up about yielding to this man in particular?

Something about it hit hot buttons she didn't know were lurking in her sexual subconscious. She felt her defenses crumbling, but she told herself it was just physical.

They both needed this.

"I like the sound of that," she confessed as the backs of her calves hit the heavy, carved side rails of the king-size bed.

Then, pinned between Ryder and the mattress covered by white pillows, Jessamyn gave in to the urge to tunnel her fingers under his T-shirt.

She ran her fingers along the ridges of his abs,

lingering briefly before she dragged the cotton up and over his shoulders. Ryder's hands followed hers, mirroring her action with her shirt until it was on the floor on top of his. He made a guttural sound of approval at her lack of bra—she'd only half paid attention to clothes this morning.

She could hardly regret the decision when the end result was his lips on her nipple all the faster, his tongue teasing circles around each taut peak, one after the other. Her breasts had never felt so exquisitely sensitive.

Winding her fingers through his thick, dark hair, she arched into his mouth, needy for more. For everything.

He seemed to understand, his hands already at work on her sweatpants, dragging them down her body along with the sleep shorts she'd been wearing underneath.

"No panties, either," he muttered darkly as he helped her out of her clothes. "Are you trying to make me lose all restraint?"

"No," she replied automatically before rethinking, her whole body tingling as he stroked a tentative touch between her thighs. Her legs went limp. She sort of collapsed into his touch. "Maybe. Yes, actually. That's my final answer."

His eyes were glowing coals when they met hers, his fingers teasing the sweetest sensations from her body.

This time, when his mouth found hers, the kiss was

a claiming. A no-holds-barred mating of tongues as they took and gave in equal measure, hungry for more.

She wrapped her arms around his neck and he lifted her onto the bed, displacing a handful of white pillows. He only paused the kiss long enough to strip off the rest of his clothes and retrieve a condom from his nightstand.

Yes, yes, yes. She thought she chanted it in her head but based on how quickly he tore off the wrapper and sheathed himself, she might have been urging him on out loud.

Either way, she knew he must get the message by the way she tilted her hips to his, seeking. She trailed kisses up his throat, reveling in the hot taste of him while she stroked her foot up his calf.

When at last he pushed his way inside her, the sensation rocked her. She hadn't realized she was already so close to orgasm from his touches. But now, feeling the warning ripples already squeezing her womb, she could only lock her ankles around his waist and hold on tight.

"Feels so good," she gasped.

"Need you," he groaned at the same moment, their words interlacing as thoroughly as their bodies.

Her fingernails dipped into the muscle along his shoulder, seeking purchase. Or maybe just hanging on to the pleasure for as long as possible.

But the tide of hunger was too strong. The next time his thumb circled the bud of her sex, she flew apart, her body gripped with delicious waves of bliss.

Her head fell back, at the mercy of the sensations while Ryder found his peak a moment later.

He gripped her hips tightly, holding her where he needed her, and she melted at the sight of him lost in the same undertow as her.

For long minutes, they held each other in the aftermath. Unlike their first time together, she didn't feel the same worry about what would happen next. Clearly, avoiding Ryder hadn't helped her to get over the attraction to him. Once hadn't been enough to get him out of her system.

How long would it take?

Opening eyes that had fallen shut, she slanted a glance over at Ryder on his back now beside her. His breathing was even, but she knew he hadn't fallen asleep. Still, he had to be exhausted from being on the mountain all night.

Her limbs felt heavy, too, her whole body limp and languid. From the incredible orgasm, she guessed. Although she'd woken up feeling tired, too, which was so unlike her.

And there'd been that weird moment of nausea this morning. Was she coming down with something? Or did she just need to eat?

"You must be starving," she reasoned, levering up on an elbow. "And tired. Would it be weird of me to volunteer to make us something to eat?"

His gaze flicked over her exposed breasts, and she couldn't help the smoky wisps of pleasure that floated through her at his attention.

"I could probably do with something more substantial than you," he teased, his eyes darkening as he kissed the rounded curve. "Then again, I haven't gotten my fill of these. Or the rest of you."

Palming her breasts, he squeezed one gently, and she relished the new, heightened sensitivity...

The thought stopped her cold.

Sensitive breasts.

Nausea.

Unusual exhaustion.

She quickly added up math that didn't compute. They'd used condoms. She was on the pill.

"Jess?" Ryder's head lifted from the sensual attention he'd been paying her body. "Something wrong?"

"I— No." She shook her head, even though a prickle of dread needled at the base of her spine. Especially when she thought about when she'd last had her period.

Back in New York. Six weeks ago?

Panic bubbled up her throat.

"Talk to me." Ryder's voice grew more urgent, his hands going to her shoulders to steady her. "What's the matter?"

Her heart raced. Her mouth felt like cotton.

"Nothing. I'm fine," she started, needing to reassure herself and failing miserably. "But I—" She swallowed hard and started again. "I should get going."

Levering herself off the bed, she bent to retrieve her T-shirt and plunged her arms into the sleeves. She needed distance from him—fast—to wrap her head around her upside-down world.

"I don't understand." He shook his head as he sat up fully, moving to the edge of the bed as he watched her with wary eyes. "Why the sudden rush?"

Pressing her hand to her head, she didn't even begin to know how to answer that.

"Just feeling a little guilty, I guess," she began again, needing to make her excuses so she could figure out a more reasonable explanation for why she was feeling off today. "I know you'd already be sleeping if not for me. You must be exhausted after the rescue."

She moved back to the bed to lay a hand on his forearm. To make him see she was okay, even though she was anything but. The warmth of his body reminded her of how recently they'd been wound around one another, finding pleasure unlike anything she'd ever known.

Hiding her thoughts from him now wasn't easy, but she needed to spare him this worry until she was certain. Until she knew what to do next.

His eyes darkened at her touch. He hooked a hand around the back of her thigh, drawing her closer so she stood between his knees.

"I was glad to see you when I got home," he admitted, his voice gravelly. "You're welcome to share my bed for as long as you like."

Her pulse skittered, her body reacting despite everything. But she bit down the response, needing to retreat before she fell any deeper under this seductive spell.

"I'll call you later." Forcing a smile, she leaned

forward to brush a kiss over his lips, wishing with all of her being that she could stay, that things could be uncomplicated between them. "You should sleep now."

Blue eyes searched hers for a long moment. Then, after he kissed her a second time with thorough, knee-melting skill, his touch slid away from her slowly.

"All right. I'll let you go." A wicked twinkle lit his gaze. "If you agree to be my guest at the Atlas Gala next weekend."

Her throat went dry. She shouldn't say yes to any such thing when they could be facing a monumental problem. When she could be carrying his child even now.

But she couldn't bring herself to tell him about that before she was certain. And perhaps it was a false alarm and she could just keep things simple between them after all. So she backed up a step and forced herself to nod.

Willing her voice to be steady, she gave him the only response that wouldn't tangle them in a longer conversation. "Of course. It's a date."

Eight

Twisted in his sheets six hours later, Ryder woke from uneasy dreams.

Spearing a hand through his hair, he winced at a muscle strain in his shoulder. He must have pulled it during the rescue when he'd leaned deep into a crevice to haul one of the panicked climbers to safety. There'd been concern among the SAR team that the guy had seriously injured his legs given his lack of movement and his symptoms of shock. He'd been pale and clammy, anxious in the extreme. He was only twenty-three, and he'd fallen in an ascent with his brother. The two of them had been trying to outdo one another on the trail, racing where they should have been spotting each other. The brother's blatant disregard for his younger sibling had reminded Ryder too much of the way Jessamyn's father had behaved during a long-ago climb, bringing back too many bad memories.

Shoving out of his bed, Ryder padded barefoot toward the en suite bathroom, then flipped on the dual-head shower. While steam rose off the Calacatta marble salvaged from a home demolition, he tried to gather his bearings and shake off the nightmares. In his sleep, his brain had confused the recent rescue with his first winter mission involving Mateo Barclay on one of Colorado's most dangerous peaks. The episode where Mateo's bravado had almost cost his then-girlfriend her life.

Ryder stepped under the powerful stream of water, hoping to wash away thoughts of the incident he'd put out of his mind until Jessamyn returned to Catamount. Yet from that day forward, it had circled his head daily since Mateo's confessions on Longs Peak might be enough evidence for the Barclay sisters to win their case. With each passing hour, keeping quiet about what he knew weighed heavier on him. Especially now that they were spending time together again. He wasn't sure what the future held for them when her life was still about the real estate business based in New York. But he felt certain the connection they shared didn't come around often. He'd let her go ten years ago to pursue her dreams, only to discover he wanted her even more now than he had back then.

Still, Jessamyn deserved to know the truth about her dad, although it would hurt her deeply.

Enough to make her cut ties with Mateo and New York?

Certainly, that wasn't any part of Ryder's motive

in wanting her to know about her father, but it was a real possibility. Shutting down the shower nozzles, Ryder stepped out of the tile shower surround to towel off, contemplating his options for giving her the information she needed. It wouldn't violate any standard of ethics if she learned the truth from Mateo's ex-girlfriend. Or better yet, straight from Mateo himself.

Tossing his towel aside, Ryder strode into the closet where built-in mahogany shelves and racks organized business and black-tie attire on one side, while deep drawers on the other side contained rescue gear and work clothes. He pulled on jeans and a long-sleeved T-shirt before returning to the bedroom to retrieve his phone.

He couldn't put this off any longer if he wanted any hope of moving forward with Jessamyn. First, he typed in the name of the woman who'd fallen during that long-ago climb with Mateo. Finding her might have been easier if she'd had a more unusual name than Susan Wilson. As it stood, the number of results was staggering, even if he limited his search to Colorado, which didn't seem realistic.

Conceding he might need to hire an investigator to find her, Ryder closed that screen and decided to go straight to the source first. He searched for a number for Mateo Barclay.

After only a second's hesitation, he punched it in and waited while it rang three times before switching over to voice mail.

Committed to his task, Ryder delivered the message he should have given Jessamyn's father weeks ago.

"Barclay, this is Ryder Wakefield from Catamount." He considered that sufficient identification. There was no way Jessamyn's father would have forgotten the man who sat with him on a brutally cold mountainside while Mateo confided his darkest secrets. "We need to talk about the Crooked Elm property before this case goes further." He halted a moment, unwilling to make ultimatums over the phone. Exhaling a frustrated breath, he said simply, "Call me back."

Disconnecting, Ryder wished that the effort had eased some of his unrest over how long he'd delayed taking this action to help Jessamyn. But a sense of disquiet remained.

He told himself it was only because she'd seemed unsettled when she'd left his house earlier. As if she'd been withholding something from him. But who was he to point fingers at her for that considering his own behavior?

Sinking into a leather armchair in the living area of his primary suite, he cracked open his laptop to work on finalizing plans for the Atlas Gala. The organizers had been sending him questions that he'd been too busy to field the past few days.

Now that he had lined up Jessamyn for his date, he was all the more committed to making sure the event ran flawlessly. He would romance her. Showcase Wakefield Ranch at its most impressive. Because if there was any chance the news about her father convinced her that life in New York wasn't for her, Ryder intended to make sure she saw Catamount, Colorado—and him—as too tempting to resist.

Unable to sit in the empty and echoing ranch house at Crooked Elm, Jessamyn sat outside at the picnic table in the backyard, watching her grandmother's long-eared goats play in their pen nearby. The three Nubian goats—Guinevere, Morgan Le Fay and Nimue—cavorted in the sunshine, kicking up their heels and making a happy racket as they romped around the enclosure.

Jessamyn had come home from Wakefield Ranch bursting at the seams to talk to Fleur, but her sister had been out with Drake Alexander. The only sign of Fleur had been a handwritten note on stationery dotted with daisies, saying that she was having a "sleepover" at Drake's place and was taking a day off from delivering her baked goods tomorrow. Fleur had stuck the note to the electronic tablet she used in the kitchen and had added a second sticky note underneath it suggesting Jessamyn touch base with Lark to update their sister about their progress on the case.

Jessamyn clutched the tablet now as she slid off the picnic table and walked toward the goat pen, unsure what progress she had to share about the will contest. She'd found very little evidence to discuss in a courtroom.

Besides, she'd been so full of her pregnancy worries that she hadn't been able to think about the will contest proceedings coming up. She'd briefly considered stopping at the local market on the way home for a pregnancy test, but Catamount was such a small town she feared the rumor mill would be full of the news before suppertime. And, maybe a little part of her feared making the news official. Once she did the test, there was no going back. It wasn't like her to avoid uncomfortable truths, but Jessamyn really didn't feel ready for baby news.

Was it foolish to cross her fingers that her period was just late? They had used two forms of contraception after all. Although in thinking about it, she recalled that she'd been on antibiotics for that spider bite around the time she'd first been with Ryder. So there was a possibility that had lowered the effectiveness of the pill.

Stopping near the fence enclosure, she watched the little black-and-white one trot over to greet her. She reached between the taut wires to stroke the animal's warm fur as she glanced down at Fleur's note again, still stuck on the tablet in Jessamyn's other hand. The news that Fleur was taking a day off from baking came as a surprise. Fleur had worked tirelessly to build her local following as a caterer and baker, hoping to launch her restaurant business on the reputation of her sought-after foods.

Also a surprise? How disappointed Jessamyn had felt about her sibling's absence. She couldn't deny that she was growing closer to Fleur, the way their grandmother had always wanted all three of them to heal their differences. In Antonia Barclay's absence,

Crooked Elm still seemed to work its old magic, making Jessamyn feel the pull of "home."

The thought of her grandmother and the wishes she hadn't lived to see fulfilled had Jessamyn pressing the button on top of the tablet, opening the screen for a video call to Lark. Not to share her pregnancy fear, but maybe just to…check in.

"I was just thinking about you—" Lark's voice sounded while her image came into view a moment behind. When the video connected, her older sister squinted at the screen. "Oh, wait. Jessamyn?"

A moment of self-consciousness made her defensive.

"Sorry to disappoint you," she snapped, straightening from where she'd been petting Nimue. "Fleur thought I should touch base to update you on the will contest case."

"Okay, sounds good." Lark stood in her closet dressed in gym clothes and looking like she'd just returned from a workout. Behind her, Jessamyn could see a selection of somber pantsuits in grays, blues and browns.

Her sister's eyes were a deep, mossy green, her dark hair a glossy braid that snaked over one shoulder. Lark was a natural beauty without trying, but she absolutely did not ever try. Jessamyn had never understood why her older sister rejected all things traditionally feminine or delicate with both hands, embracing form and function over all else.

"Honestly, I'm discouraged as we have very little." Jessamyn came straight to the point. "I've spent every free hour going through Gran's old journals and letters, hoping for concrete evidence we can use, but she only talks about the gardens and cooking. There's not much that's personal."

Lark frowned as she looked into the camera and toed off her black tennis shoes. "Surprising given how vocal she was with us about her hopes for the ranch in the future. How she wanted it to help us realize our dreams."

The disparaging note in Lark's voice caught Jessamyn off guard.

"You sound like you're not interested in coming back here." Jessamyn knew that her older sister had rarely visited Crooked Elm. Once Lark had checked out of Catamount, she was done. "Were you just humoring Fleur when you told her you'd try to visit the ranch before the end of the summer?"

Fleur had elicited a promise from both of them at Antonia's memorial service. Their younger sister had been determined to carry on their grandmother's efforts to heal their differences.

Lark grabbed a gray blazer and pants from a hanger and laid them over her arm before moving out of her closet into an all-white bedroom. "I'll be there next week. I won't miss the court case."

Vehemence underscored the words.

"I'm glad," Jessamyn told her honestly, sensing Lark would be formidable in court if she had any testimony to offer. "Will you be submitting a statement?"

"I'm working on it." Lark tossed the suit on the

crisp white blanket that served as the bed's only ornament, corners tucked so tightly a stranger might have guessed Lark had been in the military. "Have you seen my ex-husband around town since you've been there?"

"Gibson?"

The corners of Lark's lips quirked. "Thankfully, I only have one ex-husband."

Jessamyn stifled a smile. Lark was a hard-ass by anyone's standards, but she had a quiet sense of humor that could catch a person by surprise.

Los Angeles–based Lark had been briefly wed to a hockey player who—at that time—had skated for a West Coast team. Lark had been working as a sports psychologist back then, and the two had connected immediately. But the relationship wore away under the strain of Gibson's travel, according to Lark's extremely limited commentary on the marriage. And Jessamyn had only heard that much secondhand since she'd had a strained relationship with her sisters until recently.

Interestingly, Gibson had been in the process of buying a ranch close to Crooked Elm at the time of the divorce. Jessamyn had assumed that they were going to live in Catamount, but as far as she knew, Lark had never set foot in the place. Gibson, however, had been known to pop into town in the off-season, staying for two months at a time while he fixed up the place.

"Right. A good thing." Jessamyn leaned against a wooden post for the goat enclosure, setting aside her own worries to concentrate on her sister. "I haven't heard or seen Gibson in town, and I would think if the local hockey star was in residence, there would have been talk of it at the Cowboy Kitchen."

"Excellent news." Lark nodded her satisfaction as she tugged the band off her braid and began unthreading her hair. "I'll try to get my statement submitted to the attorney by the weekend so you can preview it, and I'll see you next week."

Jessamyn recognized the phrases that signaled the end of the communication and, disheartened to have made little progress on extending an olive branch to her older sister, she signed off and shut down the tablet.

Their relationship remained functional but unfulfilling, and Jessamyn wondered if Lark kept everyone at a bit of a distance anyhow. It seemed like that would be her way. Although maybe Lark thought the same thing about her.

Considering Jessamyn hadn't shared so much as a hint about her own woes, maybe that was true. But she didn't want it to be anymore. She was tired of following their father's example of having relationships serve a purpose.

She didn't want that any more than she'd wanted to marry Brandon. Returning to Catamount had reminded her she wanted deeper connections.

Just maybe not co-parenting type deep.

Her gut cramped at the thought of a possible pregnancy, and she turned the tablet on to the calendar function to count days and recalculate when her period was due.

She'd never been very regular in the first place, so she might be worrying for nothing. In the meantime, she had a lot on her plate to finish going through Antonia's boxes. She'd wait a few more days before she went rushing off two towns over to buy a pregnancy test kit.

It was early yet.

Better to put the worry—and Ryder—out of her mind.

She closed the tablet just as her phone vibrated in her back pocket.

Ryder's name appeared on the screen, but it wasn't a call.

Your tenant Josiah Cranston just showed up on the wildlife camera to check the trap.

She'd forgotten all about the illegally set trap. Anger fired through her now at the reminder. At herself for being so caught up in Ryder that she'd allowed the trapper to slip from her mind. And at the thought that their tenant was the very same person committing criminal acts on their property.

Memories of Phantom whining and scared in that snare made her determined to prosecute the one responsible.

She typed a note back to Ryder, furious fingers stabbing the screen.

Heading over there now.

Darting inside the house to retrieve the rental car's keys, Jessamyn calculated the best route to put her closest to the site. Ryder had taken the device for evidence, of course, but they'd monitored where it had been with the cameras.

Ryder's text was almost immediate.

Do NOT confront him. I'm calling the parks and wild-life department.

And risk having Cranston gone by the time they got there? At least this way, Jessamyn could be sure to find the guy in the vicinity of his wrongdoing. Maybe he would lead her to more of his illegally set ambushes.

Besides, after a day of gut-wrenching worries, the possibility of having an outlet for some of her frustrations practically pushed her into the driver's seat of her rental.

Defensiveness for Crooked Elm and her grandmother's land fueled her anger, calling her to protect this place. Not just for her, but for Fleur and Lark, who both needed the healing this place might offer.

Crooked Elm had given Fleur the gift of a fresh career path and new love. Jessamyn knew she wouldn't find either of those in Catamount since her life and work would always be in New York. If anything, Barclay Property Group would be the legacy she had to offer a child if—and it was a big if—she really did turn out to be pregnant.

But even so, life in Catamount had given Jessamyn a smaller gift that was no less wonderful. The possibility of a family in her sisters, who still might become her friends again.

Fueled by that hope, and the need to ensure Crooked Elm was a safe place for Lark to find whatever she needed from the quirky ranch where they all had roots, Jessamyn pressed the accelerator harder. The sedan bounced over the rough road, spitting gravel out the tires as she steered along an access route toward the feeder creek that led to the White River.

For a moment, she had a passing fear that all this passionate defensiveness of her home was some kind of pregnancy hormone gone wild. A nesting instinct nine months too early. But that was absurd thinking. She was overtired and letting her imagination run away with her when her period was just late.

End of story.

What was more important was that this little corner of the world had come to mean something to her. And she'd be damned if she let anyone steal the tenuous sense of peace, healing and—yes—*family* she'd found here.

Nine

By the time Ryder reached the spot in the woods where his battery-operated camera was located, two Colorado wildlife officers were already on the scene.

Ryder had spotted the government agency's Jeep on the trail closest to the creek, with Jessamyn's rented white sedan parked nearby, mud-spattered from the trip through the fields. Now, after leaving his truck on the trail, Ryder made his way toward the group standing beside the slow-running stream. The sun was setting on the summer day, the sky already more pink than gold.

Two agents in matching khaki uniforms—a slim, dark woman with steel-colored hair in a razor-sharp cut and a round-cheeked younger man with thumbs hooked in his belt—flanked Jessamyn. And it was a damned good thing they did. Because Ryder did not like the look of the grizzled rancher in dirty coveralls standing across from them.

Ryder had run into Antonia Barclay's tenant in town enough times to know Josiah Cranston was unfriendly to the point of rude. But right now, the man's pale blue eyes were narrowed in fury as he glared at Jessamyn in a way that made him seem more than just rude.

The man looked outright dangerous.

"It's against the law to film me without my consent," the rancher shouted, cords standing out from his neck as he leaned toward her. "I know my rights."

Protectiveness surged, quickening Ryder's step. He didn't trust Cranston. And why were the wildlife officers letting the guy yell at Jessamyn? Shouldn't they be intervening?

"This is my land—" Jess began calmly, her tone tougher to hear from a few yards away.

But the old-timer didn't let her finish.

"That I pay good money to use," Cranston argued, voice rising another octave as he pointed toward the camera mounted to the trunk of an old alder tree. "I have a right to privacy on this property when I'm paying rent, and that means you can't record me."

"Don't blame her, Cranston." Ryder joined the conversation as he arrived at the group. He made a place for himself between the young officer and Jessamyn, placing a protective hand at the small of her back. Or a soothing one, maybe. He wanted Jess to know he was there to give whatever help he could.

"That's my camera, and I mounted it after finding my neighbor's dog caught in your trap. The animal was fortunate we came along when we did."

Jessamyn's spine was rigid beneath his touch, and he hated that she had to listen to Josiah Cranston at all, let alone that she had to suffer him continuing to rent grazing acreage when they knew him to be a miserable guy. He'd cheated Antonia Barclay out of an irrigation system he'd promised to build in a verbal agreement in exchange for cheaper rent. More recently, he'd been ignoring conservation warnings to change his grazing practices for the sake of the wetlands, much to the frustration of Drake Alexander, who'd devoted years of hard work to improve the ground as well as the water quality of the local creeks that fed the White River.

Ryder told himself not to let the guy's anger spur his own, however. He calmed himself by breathing in the scent of Jessamyn's hair as he stood beside her.

Cranston wasn't anywhere near calm, however.

"I don't care who mounted it," the rancher continued loudly, startling a couple of birds from a branch overhead. "The fact is, I've been illegally recorded. I've been a paying tenant on this land for five years, and I know my rights." Cranston stamped his foot for emphasis as he repeated himself. "I can trap nuisance animals on my own land."

Jessamyn's already straight spine tensed further at the words. She hauled in a breath as if to take him to task. No doubt she wanted to remind him that he was using more of the Barclay lands than what he'd paid to rent, but the female officer intervened first.

"We have no record of a relocation permit for taking nuisance animals, Mr. Cranston," the woman told him, her voice neutral and her face impassive. "Furthermore, leghold traps are outlawed in this state."

"Not when it's a matter of human health and safety," Cranston roared, spittle flying. Then, swinging back toward Jessamyn, he leveled his gnarled finger at her. "And I've got permission to trap here firsthand from your daddy."

Ryder felt the jolt of surprise ripple through Jessamyn, though she hid it well. He would have been glad to settle this with Cranston himself, but he knew better than to step on Jessamyn's toes when she'd been working hard for weeks to secure the rights to Crooked Elm for her siblings.

Instead, he turned to address the female wildlife officer, whose demeanor made him guess she was the senior of the pair.

"Would it be easier for you to speak to both parties separately?" he asked, hoping it came across as a strong suggestion. At the same time, he slid his hand around Jessamyn's hip, reminding her he was beside her.

Trying his damnedest to help without interfering.

It spoke to how rattled she must be that she allowed him to take the lead. He guessed hearing her father had involved himself in her dispute with Cranston had cracked a bit more of her faith in her old man.

"That would be best." The woman's name badge

glinted in the last rays of the setting sun showing through the trees. N. Davies. "If you wait by the vehicles, we'll join you in a few minutes."

Once Jessamyn nodded, Ryder led her up the hill toward his truck, hating the way the confrontation had left her pale, her lips pursed.

"You okay?" he asked once they were out of earshot of the party near the creek.

Behind them, he could hear Cranston still ranting. But at least at a distance, the other sounds of the wooded thicket became audible. A rabbit rustling in dead leaves nearby. A dead branch creaking softly in the slight breeze.

She wrapped her arms around herself and Ryder fought the urge to wrap her in his instead.

"I'll feel better once Dad tells me that Cranston made up the part about obtaining permission to trap from him," she admitted, stopping beside his truck bed to lean on the fender. "The guy is a piece of work."

"No doubt." Ryder agreed with the latter, though he had his doubts about the former. He found it all too easy to believe Mateo Barclay had conversed with his mother's tenant in recent weeks. "And I hope you're right about your father. But it would be foolish of Cranston to make claims that would be so easy to disprove."

He propped his elbow on the ledge of the cargo box, wishing he could take her home and help her forget the unpleasantness of the day.

"Dad wouldn't do that," she told him impatiently,

straightening to reach in the back pocket of dark denim jeans to withdraw her phone. "I'm calling him so we can confirm that right now."

His gut knotted at the thought of her finding out what a creep her father was. As much as Ryder wanted her to know the truth, he hated that it would hurt her.

But before Jessamyn could dial, the younger of the two officers scrambled up the hill toward them.

"Officer Davies said you don't have to stay, ma'am." The man thumbed up the brim of his pale beige Stetson as he addressed Jessamyn. His badge read B. Jenkins. "We have a record of the complaint called in by Mr. Wakefield, and we'll write up a citation."

"You will?" Jessamyn's eyebrows lifted. "Even though my tenant says he had permission to trap?"

While she spoke, Ryder reached into his truck bed to retrieve the trap he'd confiscated the day they freed Phantom. He'd held on to it until the officers could come out to the land.

Officer Jenkins nodded, his thumbs returning to hook on his belt. "We take this sort of thing seriously. Of course, Mr. Cranston can opt to argue it in court, so it may come down to a judge's discretion. Especially if he obtained permission from Mr. Barclay."

Ryder saw Jessamyn's fists clench. Hoping to save her the aggravation of arguing the point, he passed the device to the guy. "I'd like to turn this in to you as evidence. We took it with us to keep pets and wildlife safe from potential harm."

"Sure thing. Thank you both." With a tip of his hat, the officer ambled to the Jeep, carrying the trap.

Leaving Ryder alone with Jessamyn as she rubbed her temples between her fingers and thumb.

"I think we've done all we can for today." He glanced to where Josiah Cranston still spoke emphatically to the senior officer. "Can I make you dinner tonight? I'd like to treat you to something nice to get your mind off this."

Hazel eyes snagged on his, and for a moment, he thought he saw a hint of yearning in them. But she nibbled her lip before shaking her head. "Thank you. But I really do need to speak to my father about everything that's happened with Cranston. If my dad's working against me somehow on this, too…well, I need to know what he's about."

Guilt wrenched his insides. But damn it, he wanted her to find that out. Even though it would hurt to hear, delaying would only magnify the pain.

It didn't bode well that Barclay had never phoned him back after Ryder left a message. No doubt Mateo Barclay would be just as glad for Ryder to forget about that long-ago conversation they'd had on the mountainside.

"Fair enough. How about later this week? I know you might not stick around Catamount for long after the Atlas Gala since the probate court case is on the docket for the week after that." He'd looked it up since he wasn't about to let her go into that courtroom without more evidence. Even now, his investigator was looking for Susan Wilson, who could at least offer evidence of Mateo Barclay's darker deeds. "I thought maybe we could do some of the things that we used to do together. Go hiking or horseback riding?"

Twilight had faded into near darkness while they'd been standing there, leaving them in shadows. Jessamyn's pale face was still visible, though, her eyes searching his.

"Don't you think that will complicate things unnecessarily?" She shifted on her feet uneasily.

But she hadn't said no.

"I think we could both use some fun." He was determined to keep things light. To show her they could have a good time together outside of sex.

To romance her?

Yes, exactly that.

"I guess that would be all right. I can't spend all of my free time reading Antonia's papers," she conceded. "Maybe a hike on Wednesday?"

Ryder's chest thumped with the victory. He wanted to haul her into his arms and kiss her breathless in response, but with the voices of the officers and Cranston still nearby, he refrained.

For now, her agreeing to the date would be enough.

"Sounds good." He couldn't stop himself from rubbing his hands down her arms, though. Squeezing lightly while he breathed in her amber-and-vanilla scent. "I'll see you then."

Letting her go wasn't easy, but he told himself it was only for a couple of days. Maybe by then, he'd have found a way to relate her father's misdeeds in a manner that wouldn't compromise his ethics or—he sincerely hoped—wouldn't cause Jessamyn too much pain.

Jessamyn didn't wait long to try calling her father.

After the debacle with Josiah Cranston, she drove her rental car home with more care than she'd taken on the way over there. Arriving back at the Crooked Elm main house, she lingered outdoors in the light of a pale moon, taking a seat on an old swing in the sprawling box elder tree out front.

The house was quiet behind her. Fleur must still be with Drake.

Her father answered in two rings.

"Jessamyn. We need to talk." Her father's voice was all business, like always. For years, she'd told herself she admired that about him—his way of coming to the point quickly worked to his favor in business and saved time in meetings. But tonight, when she felt shaken for too many reasons to count, she really wished he was the sort of parent who took time to ask how she was doing.

But she knew he was the same Mateo Barclay as always. It was Jessamyn who'd changed this summer. Still, she knew how to operate in his world. She was good at it.

"Indeed we do." The clipped manner of her New York speech had everything to do with content, not accent. It felt unnatural to use that language as she sat on the swing, moonlight bathing her bare calves in white light where her cropped jeans ended on her legs. "Josiah Cranston claims you gave him permission to trap on our land. Is that so?"

The extra second of silence answered her question before her dad spoke.

"What if it is? Crooked Elm is my mother's property, Jessamyn. And it should legally come to me upon her death now that her will has come into question."

Fury ripped through her at his cold about-face from the answers he'd given to her about his challenge before.

"So you've abandoned the tactic of inheriting a share of the property along with my sisters and me?" She rose from the swing to pace the driveway, her feet covering long strides to work off the angry energy. "Now you're going for the whole thing in spite of Gran's wishes?"

"My attorney says it's cleaner that way." In the background, Jessamyn could hear an evening news program. No doubt he sat in his study with his nightly glass of scotch and his review of the day's business deals. "When a woman without a spouse—like my mother—dies intestate, her property goes to her children. In this case, me."

She heard ice cubes clinking against a glass as he rattled his drink. He'd always found it hard to sit still, jingling his keys, his coins, his ice.

"But she *didn't* die intestate. You know as well as I do that Gran had a will." Jessamyn couldn't hold on to her clipped, all-business facade now. Not when her dad was threatening something that her sisters were counting on.

And now, she counted on it, too. Not that she needed the income from the estate. But because of what it signified. A place where they'd all been happy once. A home where good memories had been made.

Maybe even for her, because Catamount was where she'd first fallen in love. For the only time in her life. Her throat felt raw to think on that time and how easily she and Ryder had walked away from those early passions. Yet she'd been comparing men to him ever since.

"If the will was important to her, she would have made it ironclad," he reasoned, referring to the fact that Gran had changed the will several times over the years through an online program, not always taking the time to have her lawyer review the revisions. "Because she didn't, I will assume she intended for the estate to fall to me."

This time, it was her turn to allow an extra beat of silence as she absorbed that blow.

The revelation that her father was every bit as much of a selfish bastard as her mother and sisters had always believed him to be. Why had she refused to recognize it before now? He didn't even bother to couch his greed in more palatable terms. Didn't try to justify his actions as anything other than a money grab. Jessamyn felt like the foundation beneath her feet had fallen away. The one family member she'd always counted on to have her back didn't care for anyone but himself.

"Have you been this awful all these years, and I didn't see it until now?" How many times had her sisters told her that their father only looked out for himself?

Maybe she hadn't wanted to see it because it might mean—like her mom once told her—that Jessamyn was that selfish, too.

But she wasn't a kid anymore. And she knew that wasn't true.

"Do you think I've built Barclay Property Group by being the nicest guy in the room, Jessamyn? Or have I built it by being the smartest?"

Anger simmered hotter.

"Neither. You've built it by being ruthless. And it's one thing to be a shark in business. It's another to be that way with family." She quit pacing the driveway to look back at the house where her grandmother had built a life on her own for years after her husband died.

She'd raised goats and made cheese. She'd nurtured granddaughters when her son left the ranch to pursue his business. And she'd wanted her granddaughters to enjoy the same peace and contentment she'd found here. Even now in the moonlight, Jessamyn could see Antonia Barclay's fanciful touches. A bright orange tile inlaid with a yellow sun set into a stucco archway near the front door. Turquoise and yellow pillows spilling off a painted green bench to welcome visitors.

Arriving here was still like walking into a hug. And if there was any chance that Jessamyn carried a child, she would want to raise a baby in that kind of environment. One that felt like a hug and not a race to the fattest bottom line. She would still be proud of her legacy in real estate development, but that didn't mean she needed to live and breathe it.

"Catamount has turned you sentimental." Her father lobbed the accusation with distaste, his words dragging her back to the conversation. "Is that why you told Brandon you won't go through with the marriage? An attack of sentiment?"

Closing her eyes, she refocused on her parent, understanding at last that he didn't have her best interests at heart now. He might have, at one time. But the will contest was all about him.

"Brandon and I work well together," she told him tiredly. "We don't need to muddy our professional relationship with matrimony."

"You may need the marriage to hold on to the company, though, since I consider Brandon my heir apparent. Since the new fiscal year started, he's bringing in more business than you." More ice rattling. His glass sounded empty.

Sort of like Jessamyn's heart right now.

At one time, she might have leaped to prove him wrong. But she didn't want any part of those competitive games tonight.

"Whatever you do with the company, Dad, make sure your wishes are ironclad. You wouldn't want a conniving offspring to undermine you." She could almost hear his displeasure. Perhaps it was in the way he stopped shaking his tumbler. "I'll see you in court."

Disconnecting the call, she felt a tremor go through her at her own nerve.

No. At *his* nerve.

Because he was the one responsible for his behavior. For giving Josiah Cranston permission to trap on Barclay land that Gran had meant for her granddaughters. For trying to make Jessamyn marry his choice of husband. For undermining his own mother to obtain Crooked Elm for himself.

Jessamyn wouldn't do any of those things. And it was past time she straightened out her life and her priorities. Not just because she might be expecting a child.

Her hand skimmed over her flat belly at the thought that had shaken her earlier in the day. There might not be anything inside there. Perhaps the pregnancy scare was the universe's way of making her see what—and who—was really important in her life.

Her sisters.

Ryder?

His name bubbled to the surface of her thoughts before she had time to hold it back.

But she wasn't ready to think about that right now. Pocketing her phone, she marched toward the house to finish going through her grandmother's boxes. Because one way or another, she would make sure the Barclay patriarch didn't get his hands on Crooked Elm.

Even if she had to personally call everyone Antonia mentioned in her journals. Everyone she'd ever corresponded with. Someone out there must be familiar with what her grandmother wanted to happen when she died.

She just needed to find that person.

Ten

After days of preparing for the Atlas Gala and tracking down Mateo Barclay's ex-girlfriend, climbing Sawmill Mountain seemed like a cakewalk for Ryder.

Although it would be more enjoyable if Jessamyn would talk to him.

"We're almost there," he observed in yet another effort to draw her out.

He glanced over at Jessamyn beside him, a light-weight backpack strapped to her shoulders. The sun lit her dark hair with copper, the long strands twisted into a braid and clipped at the end with a gold clasp.

She'd seemed preoccupied ever since he'd picked her up for their hiking date, but he'd credited her distraction to thoughts of finding evidence for the case against Mateo's will contest. At least she covered the terrain with ease, keeping a brisk pace in hiking boots and khaki cargo shorts. Her legs had distracted him more than once, the sight of her bare thighs reminding him how badly he wanted them around his waist again.

Yet that wasn't all he wanted from her. Her happiness mattered to him. More than he would have expected. In fact, *she* mattered.

Was something else bugging her that she wasn't sharing with him? He tried again to nudge along conversation.

"Remember when we climbed Devil's Causeway?" he asked, drawing on an old memory.

"It was a beautiful sunrise that day," she admitted, the smallest smile curving her lips. The mint blouse she wore made her hazel eyes look greener as she met his gaze.

"I was thinking less about the sunrise and more about when I tried to impress you with how fast I could sprint up the exposed ridge." He laughed to think of how young he'd been.

How crazy about her.

"You *were* very impressive before you lost your footing near that ledge." She ducked under a low-hanging pine branch. "But who would have expected the tourist to scream at you like that for running on a trail?"

"Obviously she couldn't wait for karma to take me down and had to help it along by scaring ten years off my life with that holler." He nodded at a couple of teenage boys hiking in the other direction, their hats pulled low to ward off the sun of a bright day.

"Good thing your catlike reflexes kicked in just in time," she teased, flipping her dark braid behind her shoulder. "You escaped with just a scratch on your knee."

"Which you nursed very tenderly, now that I think about it." He recalled sitting with her at the end of the ridge overlooking the Flat Tops Wilderness. She'd poured water from her insulated bottle over the cut and then grazed her lips over his mouth until he forgot everything but her. "Definitely worth risking my neck."

She ducked her head as if to study the trail in front of her feet, but he thought he'd seen a trace of a smile before she went quiet again.

Could it really be the court case causing her so much distraction?

He wondered if he should bring up Susan Wilson over the picnic lunch he'd planned, or if he should simply wait for Mateo Barclay's ex-girlfriend to get in touch with Jessamyn as she'd promised. He was still mulling over his best course of action when they cleared the trees to step onto the summit of the mountain. Here, a rocky outcropping offered a view of the wilderness and the creek that fed a nearby reservoir, the water glittering blue under the clear sky.

Ryder breathed deep, pulling in the fresh air along with new optimism that a picnic would put Jessamyn at ease enough to confide in him whatever was bothering her. His plan to romance her necessitated another date. Another chance to remind her how good they were together. While attending the Atlas Gala with her would be an opportunity to pull out all the stops, he feared it could mark the end of their time together unless he gave her a reason to spend longer in Catamount.

"Should we lay out the blanket under that tree?" He pointed to a cluster of lodgepole pines providing a patch of shade.

The trail was quiet aside from the teens they'd passed on the way up, and for now they had the summit area to themselves. Plus, the pines were situated away from the best view the peak offered, so they wouldn't be in the way of other hikers.

At her silent nod, they worked in tandem to drape a bright blue quilt over the pine-needle-covered sand. Then she helped him unload the food he'd brought in his pack—lobster rolls he'd special-ordered, a light salad, peach handheld pies that were one of her sister's most popular bakery items.

To top it off, mint iced tea. And he'd brought real china and silverware for the occasion so he could make the settings elaborate. Memorable. He hoped.

"Ryder, this is beautiful," she acknowledged as he handed her a white linen napkin. "You've gone to so much effort."

They settled beside one another to eat, and he hoped the tense, quiet mood might lift now.

"My pleasure. I remember how much you used to love hiking."

"I forgot how much I enjoyed it," she said as she

filled her plate, her attention straying to a blue butterfly moving through a patch of wildflowers. "I have a good life in New York, but it's very focused on work."

Taking a bite of his lobster roll, he tried not to think about how close she'd come to hitching herself to a colleague for the sake of business, but the thought of the other guy still darkened his mood a fraction.

"And you're still enjoying the job?"

She smoothed the napkin over her lap, finger tracing the stitching on the edge. "I thought I was. But lately I wonder if I've just been using work as an escape mechanism for other areas of my life where I'm less successful."

His fork stalled on the way to his mouth. Could this be why she'd been withdrawn today? He forced himself to think carefully about his response before he spoke.

"Tough to picture you failing at anything you set your mind to. You're one of the most driven people I've ever met." And that was saying a lot considering the passion he'd seen people put into search and rescue.

She sipped her tea from one of the insulated tumblers he'd brought to keep the drinks cold. "Professionally speaking, maybe. Not so much personally."

Surprised to hear her speak so candidly about perceived shortcomings, he wondered what she referred to specifically. Was it insensitive to push her for answers? A meadowlark sang sweetly in the nearby tall grass while he thought over the best response.

"I hope you're not referring to your family," he replied finally. "Because your parents bear a lot of the burden for expecting you and your sisters to choose sides."

Of course, he ascribed more of that blame to Mateo Barclay, but he was still uneasy telling her that. She'd know the truth about him soon enough.

Shrugging, she chased an arugula leaf around her plate before spearing it with her fork. "I regret not making more of an effort to patch things up with them long before now. I should have prioritized that. It's occurred to me recently that family should be—"

Stopping herself, she looked up at him quickly with an unreadable expression.

"What?" he prompted, feeling like he was missing something today.

"I've just realized that I want to place more importance on family," she finished.

Her bare knee grazed his denim-covered thigh as she repositioned herself to get more comfortable. He wanted to haul her into his lap and feed her himself before he feasted on her lips. But he knew he needed to focus on learning what was troubling her.

Before he could speak, though, she returned her attention to her meal.

"Thanks again for the picnic." She spoke in a rush in a transparent effort to change the subject.

Which was fine with him since he hadn't been able to glean what was unsettling her from that line of conversation anyhow.

"Still trying to impress you," he admitted, his eyes roaming over her face, searching for clues to her peculiar mood. "Just like on that Devil's Causeway climb."

"It's working." She licked her thumb after a bite of her lobster roll. "This is delicious."

His gaze stuck on her still-glistening thumb for a moment before he dragged his attention back to her face.

"Is everything all right? I keep thinking things seem a little...off somehow today."

Hazel eyes shot to his. For a moment, she almost looked...

Panicked?

"Jessie?" The former nickname slid from his lips without a second thought. The old care for her was still there, too. And he hated to see her troubled. "What's wrong?"

She pushed her plate aside. Knotted her napkin in one fist.

"I've been trying to find the right time to tell you," she began. "But I guess there's no perfect way to do this."

Was she leaving Catamount sooner than he'd anticipated? Breaking things off with him before he'd even had the chance to woo her at the Atlas Gala? Wary of whatever announcement she needed to make, Ryder slid his plate out of the way as well, focused on her.

"No need to couch your words with me. I can handle it." He sure as hell hoped he could, anyway.

She gave a brusque nod, her braid falling forward

over her shoulder again. The little meadowlark that had been in the grass near them trilled again, giving Jessamyn's words an unexpected drumroll.

Licking her lips, she met his gaze. "I took a pregnancy test last night, Ryder."

The words were so unexpected he figured he'd misheard. They made no sense for long, slow seconds.

"Excuse me?" he said finally, his heartbeat quickening.

"I missed my period and was worried that somehow—" She shook her head impatiently before blurting, "Look, there are no two ways about it. I'm pregnant."

Impossible.

Ryder thought it, but at least he had the wherewithal not to say it out loud.

Heart banging like off-tempo cymbals, he stared dumbfounded at Jessamyn. Just a couple of minutes ago he'd been worried she was distracted. Now that he'd learned *why,* he couldn't believe she'd kept silent about it all this time.

He was used to Jessamyn being relentlessly forthright. Candid. And she expected the same honesty from the people around her. A thought that caused him another, unrelated pang considering his own secret. He forced himself to refocus on her revelation.

"We were careful, though," he reminded her, his brain unable to wrap around this bombshell. "Weren't we?"

"I realize we used condoms, and I was on the pill." She nodded quickly, straightening the leftover dishes from their picnic. "That's why I wasn't worried at first when I was late. But it occurred to me later that I was on antibiotics briefly after that spider bite."

He recalled the day he'd seen her at the Cowboy Kitchen and she'd had a bandage on her hand.

The same day he'd taken her to the yurt and they'd ended up tearing each other's clothes off. Guilt at not protecting her better speared through him. He'd thought he'd taken care of her.

"Even so, we used condoms," he reminded himself more than her, recognizing he was too rattled to weigh in intelligently on this news. "So if one failed, the other works. That's the whole point."

She quit packing up the dishes to frown at him.

"I'm totally familiar with the process," she snapped, folding her arms across her midsection where—wow—she was now telling him his child could potentially reside.

He closed his eyes, warning himself to pull it together fast for her sake. Later, he could figure out how he felt about all this. Right now, he needed to be there for Jessamyn.

Of course she was every bit as stressed about this possibility as him.

"I realize that," he conceded. "I'm sorry I'm not processing this quickly enough."

He needed action. Movement. A way to show her his support.

A marriage proposal was the only answer in his mind. And he was about to ask her to cement their relationship that way when she spoke.

"I understand." Her tone gentled, her hazel eyes turning warm. Kind. "I already went through the denial stage, so I can hardly blame you for a knee-jerk reaction that is completely relatable."

Grateful for her easy forgiveness when his first reaction had been less than stellar, he shoved aside the open backpack she'd been refilling for their trip down the mountain and edged closer to her on the picnic blanket. As he took her hands in his, he wanted to get this next part right. He wasn't about to leave her with the burden of his child. He knew his obligation. If anything, he was grateful that she'd discovered she was pregnant while she was still in Catamount, where he could at least learn the news in person.

"Thank you. But it wasn't denial so much as surprise. I promise you I will be by your side every step of the way—"

He stopped himself since she was already shaking her head. Withdrawing her hand from his.

"That's not necessary, Ryder. I've had time to think about it, and I'm ready to take full responsibility for this child." She met his gaze directly. "I'd be glad to assume sole custody."

Judging by Ryder's expression, Jessamyn guessed she hadn't handled any part of relating the baby news well.

A blue vein ticked in his temple. A light throb of a fast, furious pulse. She'd meant to relieve him of responsibility, not frustrate him more, but she guessed that was all she'd managed to accomplish with her suggestion.

"No." His answer was the sharpest he'd ever spoken to her. "That is completely unacceptable to me. I want to be a part of our child's life, Jess. I *will* be."

Huffing out a sigh of frustration, Jessamyn rose to her feet and shouldered her small pack so they could begin the trek down Sawmill Mountain.

"Certainly you have the right if you wish—"

He was on his feet a moment after her, his expression tight as he gathered the remaining items from their abandoned picnic, rolling the blanket into a haphazard bundle and stuffing it into his pack. "I do wish. Hell, I demand it."

Nearby, voices sounded as another party of three hikers—two older women and a teenage girl—broke through the trees to the summit, delaying Jessamyn's answer.

Perhaps it was just as well that they each had a moment to regain composure. Silently Ryder zipped up his backpack for their descent.

Wishing she'd waited until they'd finished their picnic to share her news, Jessamyn headed for the trail to lead them back down to where they'd parked. She nodded at the new arrivals on her way past them. A moment later, she heard Ryder's heavier steps behind her as he caught up.

She knew perfectly well that a baby bombshell wasn't what he'd been expecting on a hiking date. So she didn't blame him for being caught off guard. She understood all too well that he must be reeling, the same way she'd been when she took that pregnancy test alone in her bathroom last night.

Then again, she'd had a few days before the test to roll the idea around in her mind. To rail against the possibility and debate what it might mean. To think about changes she'd have to make to her life to accommodate a child.

Ryder was having to condense all those reactions into seconds instead of days. Plus, he was forced to experience those responses in front of her, whereas at least she'd been able to digest it privately.

Turning on the heel of her hiking boot, she glanced back at him striding down the trail behind her, greenery slapping his legs as he passed.

"I'm sorry—"

"I'm sorry—"

They began at the same time.

It was enough to make them both smile. A moment to ease the thick tension.

"You first," he urged, quickening his pace to match hers where the trail was wide enough to walk two astride. There were only a few places that required climbing or walking one behind the other.

"I only wanted to say that you can be a part of your child's life. I didn't mean to suggest otherwise." She swatted a deerfly from her forehead as the sun sank lower on the horizon.

"Thank you." He sounded relieved. Sincere. "Can we stop for a second?"

He took her hand, and she pivoted to face him, following him to sit on a moss-covered fallen tree beside the trail. She couldn't deny the small thrill she took from having his palm wrapped around hers, his thumb stroking the back of her hand.

"We can. But considering that you just found out about the baby, I wonder if it would be wisest of us to table any discussions until you've had more time to get used to the idea?" She hadn't really thought through how awkward it might be to share the news while hiking today. She'd only known she couldn't delay relating something that affected him deeply.

"This isn't about the baby." His blue eyes looked indigo in the sunlight, his focus all on her. "This is about us."

His words seemed to reverberate through her, the deep tone of his voice almost a caress as she sat inches from him on the fallen oak.

"Us." The word whispered from her a little too softly and she could hear something in it that sounded almost wistful. So she blustered on, hoping to cover up the telltale note in her voice earlier. "You mean shared parenting? Because we should probably wait to think about that, too."

"Nothing like that." He reached for her free hand and took that one in his other palm so they sat with both sets of fingers laced. Nearby a stream babbled a soft tune. "I know this is unexpected, but considering the monumental life change we're facing, I'd like to ask you to marry me, Jessamyn."

Shock robbed her of speech.

It was her turn to search for words that wouldn't come. Her turn to reel with news she hadn't prepared for. He was only suggesting this because of the baby, of course. But there was a part of her—the old, sentimental part that had fallen for him ten years ago— that swooned a little at the idea.

And how dangerous was it to feel that way when she needed to keep her wits about her with a baby on the way? Frustration tensed her shoulders.

"Ryder—"

"Please. I want you to think about how much we cared about one another once." Releasing her hands, he moved to cup her shoulders so that they faced each other full on where they sat. "How close we came to committing ourselves to each other."

Her pulse stuttered at the mention of caring for her in the past tense. As if his feelings for her had faded long before now.

"That was a decade ago," she protested, her heart speeding in response to words that sounded almost romantic when they needed to be practical. She'd learned to guard her heart against this man the first time he'd walked away from her. It was a lesson she would need more than ever now, with a child's future at stake. "And it fell apart in the most painful way imaginable for me."

She got to her feet, surprised to realize she was a little unsteady. She steadied herself on a tree trunk before charging forward.

"Jessamyn, wait."

"No." She called on all her defenses to stay strong in the face of Ryder Wakefield's appeal. "We knew all along this was temporary between us. We're not a couple because we didn't have anything in common back then, and nothing's changed."

"A baby changes everything."

"Not what we want out of life. You're still rooted deep in Catamount, and I'm still committed to making my mark on the world in my father's business." She knew now that her father wasn't as trustworthy as she'd once believed, but that didn't make Barclay Property Group any less important to her. She'd poured her heart and soul into making the company a success. "Now it's not only about what I want to achieve. It's about creating a legacy I can be proud of to pass on to my child."

Just saying the words still felt surreal. But she needed to get used to this new turn her life had taken.

"We have plenty of things in common," he fired back. "And we can find compromises where we don't."

"Not on the big issues." She shook her head sadly, her heart aching at the thought of leaving Ryder behind again when she returned home after that will contest case. "Compromise isn't going to make New York a realistic place for you to run your ranch any more than Catamount is a potential home for a woman with an international business based in Manhattan."

A breeze stirred the leaves of the aspens overhead and one floated down to land on Ryder's broad shoulder. She smoothed it away, her fingers drawn to him even when they argued.

He tipped her chin up to his face.

"Four weeks ago you were contemplating marriage to a man for business purposes, but you won't consider marriage to me for the sake of a child?" Blue eyes bore into hers.

"You told me I'd be selling out if I wasn't marrying for love," she reminded him, even though his words stung. Her chest ached with too many emotions crowding inside. "And I decided to take your advice. Then, and now."

This time when she turned to walk the rest of the way down the mountain, Ryder didn't stop her.

She knew they still had a lot of decisions to make between them, but she was relieved to have the baby news out in the open. It was real now. Ryder knew about it.

They could decide from here what was practical.

And Ryder would quit offering up empty gestures that would only shred at her heart for all they would never have.

Eleven

"You're carrying Ryder Wakefield's baby?"

Fleur, seated on the end of Jessamyn's bed in the small bedroom at Crooked Elm, repeated the words slowly back to Jessamyn as if to ensure she had them exactly right.

The day after her hike with Ryder, Jessamyn stood in front of the room's cheval mirror, dressed in a plain black cocktail dress that seemed all wrong for the Atlas Gala. She'd been waffling over outfits for the event, torn between longing to dazzle Ryder and not wanting to look as though she'd tried too hard. Perhaps she was being a little too prideful to want her dress to slay when she walked into the event, but some part of her feminine self-confidence had taken a hit when Ryder hadn't even hinted at deeper feelings for her in his perfunctory marriage proposal.

So a black cocktail dress would not do. She reached around to her back to unzip.

"That is correct. I'm pregnant. He's the dad." While she tried on outfits, she'd decided to give her sister a bare-bones recap of the huge development in her life and how things stood with Ryder. Because soon enough, people would learn of Jessamyn's pregnancy, and she needed to get comfortable with sharing some details about that and the inevitable questions that would follow about her baby's father. "I'm only four weeks along, so maybe that's too early to broadcast the news. But it's very much on my mind, to the detriment of everything else I'm supposed to be focused on. Such as the court case."

She should have been reading more documents now, in fact, but she hadn't been able to concentrate on the cache of old letters Antonia had written. Instead, she'd been thinking about Ryder and how radically their relationship was about to change from exploring their attraction to consulting each other about nap times and nanny qualifications. Skipping right over the opportunity to develop deeper feelings for each other. The way she feared she already had for him. Was that why it had stung her so much when he hadn't seemed the least little bit optimistic about proposing to her? Because he hadn't felt the emotional tug of their relationship the way she had?

She shouldn't have been surprised, given the way

he'd walked away from her a decade ago, too. Apparently she never learned.

Unwilling to spiral into anxiety and sadness over a relationship that seemed destined not to blossom into more, she'd come upstairs to try on gowns for the gala instead. Fleur had followed, quizzing her about why she'd seemed so distracted. Making Jessamyn realize just how grateful she was for her sister's presence and support.

Shimmying off one strap of the black taffeta, she would have reached for the next hanger on the heavy iron hook installed on the back of the bathroom door. But Fleur threw her arms around her before Jessamyn could grab the garment.

"Jess, that's amazing! I'm so happy for you." Fleur's copper-colored hair tickled Jessamyn's nose as her sibling squeezed her tight. "A baby." She breathed the word reverently. "Wow. Gran would have been so thrilled about this."

For a moment, Jessamyn relaxed into the unexpected jolt of love and familiarity for her sister. Nostalgia for the way they'd once been enveloped her along with Fleur's roses-and-vanilla fragrance. The slender arms and graceful figure that had won Fleur Miss Rodeo crowns all over the West when she'd had to finance her own college tuition. Fleur's beauty and grit had taken her from scrappy fighter to accomplished woman with a rapidly growing business of her own. And Jessamyn couldn't be prouder of her.

How long had it been since they'd connected—really connected—like sisters? One old ache in her heart soothed away, a new world of possibility crowding out the hurt.

"Thank you," Jessamyn told her sincerely, her voice a little wobbly as they let go of each other. "I've been so busy worrying about the logistics of the pregnancy and what it means that I haven't taken any time to celebrate."

Taking a step back, Fleur lifted one eyebrow as she studied her. "But Ryder must be excited about it?"

Was he?

Jessamyn had been too nervous about sharing the news with him to properly gauge his reaction. Then, just when she'd been relaxed enough with Ryder to turn their baby discussion toward practical elements like how to share custody, he'd stunned her with a marriage proposal that had been purely utilitarian.

How ironic for him to seek marriage with her when he had been *adamant* that she not wed someone else for business reasons. Besides, her parents' unhappy marriage had caused her and her sisters so much grief and upheaval. She wanted better for her baby, which meant she'd need to proceed carefully with Ryder.

"I think he's still adjusting to the idea, too," Jessamyn explained carefully, turning to retrieve a pale green crepe-and-sequin gown she'd special-ordered along with three other dress possibilities for the gala.

After she stepped out of the black taffeta, Fleur rehung the piece while Jessamyn slid into the new outfit.

"I saw the way Ryder looked at you that day he came into the Cowboy Kitchen. And it was just the same way he looked at you during the summer you two were dating." Fleur rezipped the taffeta dress before turning around to help Jessamyn with the hook-and-eye closure on the crepe gown.

"Yes, well, chemistry has never been an issue between us," she acknowledged as she straightened slender tulle straps embellished with lustrous faux pearls and beads. "That doesn't mean he's ready to celebrate co-parenting with me."

She didn't mention the half-hearted marriage proposal as it didn't seem relevant. Even though she'd been thinking about that today as much as the pregnancy.

Why had he suggested such a thing when he didn't love her even a little? Were his values so traditional that he thought parents should be married to raise a child? Had he assumed she *expected* him to propose? She wished she'd thought to ask him his reason, but she'd been too shocked at the turn in the conversation.

Fleur's hands moved to Jessamyn's shoulders as Fleur stood behind her, both looking into the old cheval mirror, the glass a bit cloudy from age. "Don't discount chemistry. Ever consider that it exists to help direct you toward people who might be The One? Sort of like nature's version of a flashing neon sign that says Potential Mate?"

"Seriously?" Jessamyn laughed, pivoting on her heel to face her sister. "Lust is the new love?"

"Well, maybe not exactly that." Fleur shrugged as she turned a critical eye over Jessamyn's gown, straightening the draping at the neckline. "All I know is that I had it with Drake forever, but neither of us would acknowledge it. So for years, all of the misplaced chemistry turned into arguments and sniping."

"I remember how much you two bickered." Jessamyn watched Fleur closely, curious about how her sister had navigated confusing romantic waters. "When did you realize there was more to it?"

The transformation in her sister's expression about took Jessamyn's breath away. One moment Fleur was straightening a dress. The next, she practically glowed with giddy love.

"It was a shared horseback ride." Her cheeks even turned the slightest bit pink. Another minute and Jessamyn figured her sister's eyes would go heart-shaped. "There was an almost kiss during that ride that was…well…" Fleur fanned herself. "Suffice it to say some close proximity alerted me to a wealth of feelings that were all wrong for a guy who was supposedly my enemy."

"I can't believe you're blushing like a sixteen-year-old," Jessamyn teased, although truthfully she felt a sharp pang of envy for the obvious love Fleur had for Drake. "And I'm really happy for you. But Ryder and I—we've been down this road before ten years ago and it didn't work out then, either. I think he's too practical to consider me a romantic prospect."

"*He's* the practical one?" Fleur's eyes went comically wide. "Okay, that's saying something, coming from you when your lists have lists. Last I knew, you've never veered from a goal or a task once it's on paper."

Defensiveness straightened her shoulders and she spun away from Fleur to assess the gown in the mirror again. "Professionally, that's not a bad quality to have."

"Agreed," Fleur offered more gently, taking a step forward to stand by the reflective glass so Jessamyn had no choice but to see her. "I'm just saying that maybe you're both being so careful that you're not seeing the romantic possibilities. And since you're having a baby together—honestly—why not consider them?"

The defensiveness deflated right out of her at the wise words, delivered with nothing but kindness. Jessamyn nibbled her lip, considering.

Fleur held up a hand. "No need to answer. Just think about it. This gown is the one, by the way," she added, perhaps guessing that Jessamyn needed processing time for the deeper questions on her mind. "You're a total knockout in it, and Ryder will *not* be thinking practical thoughts when he sees you in this. If that's what you're going for."

Jessamyn glanced from her reflection in the mirror to her sibling, who stood with arms crossed over her pink apron, which said Kiss the Cook.

"That is sort of what I was going for," she confessed. "I really have no idea where to go from here with Ryder or how to handle this pregnancy. But I definitely want to look good."

Fleur winked. "That's one task you can check off the list."

Grinning, she was about to ask for Fleur's opinion on shoes when her cell phone buzzed.

"Susan Wilson." Reading the name aloud, she would have let it go to voice mail, but Fleur gripped her arm.

Halting her.

"Oh my God. That's Dad's old girlfriend," Fleur reminded her, voice lowered while the phone vibrated again. "The woman who was injured hiking with him."

"The same girlfriend who broke up with him while she was still in the hospital?" Jessamyn started to ask, but her words faded as she recalled the source of her information about that breakup—her father.

Her self-serving father.

Was there a chance Mateo Barclay had told Jessamyn a skewed version of those events? She needed to get it through her head that her dad was not the man she had believed him to be.

And didn't she want to hear from people who might know more about the Barclay patriarch as the will contest case began next week?

Taking a deep breath, Jessamyn swiped to answer the call.

"Congratulations on a stellar turnout, Ryder." Drake Alexander shook his hand. The two men stood on the red carpet that led into the event tent outside Wakefield Ranch's main house on the night of the Atlas Gala. "Although I have to admit, I thought Jessamyn would be on your arm tonight after the way you two have been circling each other these last few weeks."

Ryder straightened an obsidian horseshoe-shaped cuff link as he peered through the crowd inside the specially constructed venue for the Atlas Foundation's annual black-tie evening. Everything had kicked off as planned. The caterers had been on-site all day, including Fleur Barclay, who he'd insisted be in charge of tapas for the appetizers course of the meal. The charity's event organizer had taken on the brunt of the work throughout the day to prepare the space, but Ryder had double-checked things for himself since Wakefield Ranch would be showcased as a model of ranch-style sustainable living.

He'd long wanted to show that raising cattle could be managed with respect to the animals and the land alike, and he was proud of his efforts here. The only thing missing in an otherwise perfect evening to cap off his accomplishments?

Jessamyn. The mother of his child. The notion still leveled him.

And filled him with a protectiveness that had him awake every night thinking through how to best provide a good future for their child.

"She'll be here any minute, I expect." Ryder had faith in that, as Jessamyn Barclay was not a woman who backed out of her commitments.

He just wished he hadn't spooked her with the marriage proposal on their hike earlier in the week. Afterward, he backed off, remembering the way she'd needed space when she'd first arrived in Catamount. He'd given it to her, and she'd come around eventually, throwing over her almost fiancé to spend time with Ryder instead.

But had that approach backfired this time? It didn't bode well that he hadn't heard from her since their outing to Sawmill Mountain. Had he lost any chance he might have had of pressing the marriage question to his advantage? The thought had kept him awake every night—even more so than the fact that Jessamyn carried his baby. Because how could he even think about raising a child until he'd done everything necessary to make the mother secure?

And damn it, when was she going to show tonight? He refrained from checking his watch, aware that the cocktail hour was still in full swing and that guests were still arriving.

"Have you heard anything more about Josiah Cranston's citation from the parks and wildlife department? I don't suppose there's any chance that will set a fire under him to vacate the Crooked Elm rangelands," Drake muttered darkly, drawing Ryder's thoughts away from Jessamyn where they tended to dwell the majority of time.

On the far side of the open-air tent, chamber musicians swapped their elegant classical numbers for a spirited country tune that earned a few appreciative whistles from the cocktail hour crowd. Waitstaff were busy passing Fleur's tapas as hors d'oeuvres, trays emptying quickly. He glimpsed her across the room overseeing the presentation. And something hit him as he saw the glance—both tender and lustful—that she shot to Drake.

"I rode by his place two nights ago," Ryder admitted as he waved to one of the Atlas Foundation's founders and her husband, a couple who'd provided him with encouragement throughout his efforts to transform Wakefield Ranch. "But his truck was still there along with his equipment, so it didn't look like he'd made plans to leave anytime soon."

He didn't mention he'd only made the trip over to Crooked Elm in the hope of running into Jessamyn. His gaze flicked up to check for her arrival again.

Drake waved off a server's offer of champagne. "Maybe we won't get Cranston to budge until after the court case and ownership of the ranch is definitely awarded. I just hope the Barclay sisters win their fair due."

Surprised at the bitterness threading through his friend's voice, Ryder hauled his full attention back to Drake.

"Spoken like a man who knew Antonia was going to leave her land to her granddaughters. Are you going to be able to take the stand to that effect next week?" Ryder had been hoping he wouldn't have to test the legality of doctor-patient confidentiality. While that protection extended to EMS workers, which Ryder technically had been on Longs Peak nine years ago, there was a gray area about what kinds of information could be protected. It's not like he'd share Mateo Barclay's health history, which was strictly safeguarded by law.

But an admission made while he was in shock? An ambiguous set of circumstances as far as ethics were concerned.

So if Drake knew something that would keep Ryder from having to come forward, that would be a huge win.

"I believe so." Drake lowered his voice as a four-some of gala ticket holders arrived on the event's red carpet, shaking hands with various organizers before giving their names at the check-in table. "I submitted a statement of support. I confirmed her healthy state of mind and that her granddaughters never had undue influence over her. And I told the lawyers that when I offered to buy Crooked Elm one day, she'd laughed and said I'd need to deal with her granddaughters."

"That sounds definitive to me." Ryder's gaze shifted away from the event under the tent where the sounds of laughter, music and glasses clinking in celebration had grown in the past ten minutes. Instead, he looked down the access road leading into the ranch, hoping for a sign of Jessamyn. "I would think that weighs strongly in favor of the sisters over Mateo."

"It would carry more weight if I weren't already involved with Fleur, or if anyone else could offer similar evidence." Drake stopped one of the servers passing *croquetas de jamón* and took two along with a napkin. "But apparently I'm the only one Jessamyn has located who heard that straight from Antonia herself."

Right. And if she couldn't find anyone else, Ryder needed to step up regardless of the potential conflict of interest. He wouldn't allow her father to squeeze her out of an inheritance that rightfully belonged to her and her sisters. His obligation to speak out had doubled now that Jessamyn carried a child who would have a stake in Crooked Elm, too. He owed it to their baby to secure the rightful legacy.

"She'll find more evidence," Ryder assured him just as he spotted a familiar white rental car rolling to a stop in front of the valet stand.

Jessamyn.

Anticipation fired through him, even as he knew he'd have to come clean with her tonight. Tell her everything about that conversation with her father, offer to give evidence about his own knowledge of what Antonia Barclay intended for Crooked Elm.

Only then would he be able to turn his attention toward convincing Jessamyn to marry him. And bottom line, that was his number one objective this evening.

He couldn't imagine having his child out in the world somewhere without him. He needed to be at Jessamyn's side to raise their child together. And he knew her well enough to know that, deep down, she wanted that, too. They shared those values.

You didn't fall for someone at nineteen years old and not understand some key things about their character. Jessamyn was a family-oriented person whether she wanted to admit it or not. Now, he just needed to convince her that he was, too.

Yet, as Jessamyn stepped from her automobile, all thoughts of babies and values faded to the back of his mind.

She pivoted on her heel, sunlight catching her sequin-covered dress in a way that cast prisms everywhere. Her own personal special effects lighting that followed her wherever she went. And never had a woman been more worthy of a spotlight.

Dressed in a pale green gown that skimmed her curves like a lover's hand, darting in at her waist and hugging both her hips and her breasts, she was a vision that took his breath away. A high slit gave him glimpses of her toned thigh as she strode up the red carpet toward him. Silver, strappy heels elevated her already tall frame, giving her an elegant presence to go with her confident walk. By the time his gaze made it up to her face, framed by a dark tumble of glossy curls, he was already moving forward to meet her.

Vaguely, he heard Drake give a low whistle of appreciation. But knowing Drake, that ode to how good Jessamyn looked was most certainly just to needle Ryder. As if anything could distract him from intercepting her.

When he was a step away, he held his arms out to her, kissing her cheek.

"Wow." He breathed the word into her ear after the kiss, holding on to her a moment longer than was strictly polite. "You look good enough to eat."

He felt her cheekbone shift against the side of his face and hoped that she'd smiled. Her amber-and-vanilla fragrance called him to seek out a taste of her. To trace his tongue over the places she'd spritzed the scent that teased him.

"Thank you. But you should probably let go before you cause a scene." She didn't sound overly concerned, however.

For that, he was grateful. Tonight would be difficult enough for them both when he confided what he knew about her dad. He didn't want to go into the evening with her already keeping her guard up around him.

He longed to ask if she'd reconsidered his marriage proposal, but of course, that would have to wait. First, they needed to get through the gala.

"Didn't you hear I'm Captain Earth tonight?" he returned, squeezing her waist briefly before finally releasing her. "The title should come with a few extra privileges."

He held his arm out to her to escort her into the gala now that the event was in full swing. Jessamyn slipped her fingers around his biceps.

Only then did he truly meet her hazel eyes and see the subtle glint in them. For a moment, he glimpsed the Jessamyn Barclay who'd challenged him at the rental car kiosk weeks ago, a woman with her guard up.

"And so it does come with privileges." There was an edge to her words. "I'm still your date tonight even though our time together should be sitting down to make practical plans for our baby."

All at once, he guessed that he shouldn't have given her space. He should have shown up at her door every day to discuss the huge change in their lives that neither one of them had anticipated.

"Jessamyn." He stopped on the red carpet, his dress shoes grinding to a halt. He was unwilling to enter the event when they needed to discuss this first. "I already planned to speak to you after the gala—"

"And we will talk." She smiled with a cool politeness that told him he'd have a long way to go to convince her to marry him. He already missed the warmth of the connection they'd shared right up until she'd told him she was pregnant and he reacted in all the wrong ways. "Just not right now. We've both earned an evening of fun after a difficult week. We may as well make the most of it."

Around them, the volume of the party spilling out into the evening was increasing. The chamber musicians had given up the platform to a country rock band who were already launching into their first tune and attracting couples to a dance floor lit by twinkling blue and yellow lights hung in the rafters to look like fireflies.

Tours of his house were being given to select parties throughout the evening. But he couldn't enjoy a moment if she was unhappy.

"Let's discuss this now." He laced his fingers through hers and pulled the back of her hand to his lips so he could place a kiss there. "Nothing is more important to me than ensuring we're on the same page for our child's future."

Some of the steel left her spine at his words.

"Thank you." She gave a nod of acknowledgment. An acceptance, perhaps. "But after the gala is soon enough. For what it's worth, I am proud of you and what you've accomplished here, Ryder. Let's celebrate that first, and then we'll work through the rest."

The kindness in her eyes—the willingness to compromise—touched him deeply. And in that moment, he recalled all the reasons he'd fallen hard for her ten years ago.

Jessamyn Barclay was a woman of substance. A fiercely independent, loyal, strong person, and any man who could attract her would be beyond fortunate to keep her.

Yet as he walked through the Atlas Gala with the most beautiful woman in the room on his arm, he feared he didn't stand a chance with her. Not when he'd withheld what he knew about her father for this long. Maybe if he'd been up-front earlier, things could have been different. But he'd screwed up. Royally. How would he ever persuade her to trust him now?

What a time to realize that he loved her. Right when he was poised to lose her forever.

Twelve

"Champagne?" A bright-eyed server with a curly ponytail presented a tray of crystal flutes to Jessamyn.

Nearly two hours into the Atlas Gala, Jessamyn had her first moment alone after spending most of the time at the side of her highly sought-after date. As a host of the event, Ryder had been in demand all evening by guests interested in both his sustainable home and ranching practices. Her appreciation for his work at Wakefield Ranch had only grown as she'd listened to him explain the systems for reducing water use, recovering rainwater and sourcing gray water for irrigation. And that was just the beginning. He'd harnessed sun and wind energy in ways that made the ranch far less reliant on fossil fuel, and his efforts were attracting nationwide attention.

What woman wouldn't have been proud to be at Ryder's side this evening? Then, there'd been the way his hand had frequently sought the base of her spine as he'd guided her from one group of guests to the next, the warmth of his touch an ever-present reminder of the connection they'd shared. Throughout the night, he'd included her in conversations, given weight to her thoughts, highlighted her experience. It was obvious he respected her as well as liked her.

And she watched carefully as he interacted with his brother and sister-in-law. He cared about his family and enjoyed celebrating with them. He'd be a good father, caring and concerned. Much more than her own had ever been.

Could this connection grow into something more for the sake of their child, the way Fleur had suggested? Jessamyn found herself considering it more and more as the evening wore on, especially now as she stood alone near the chocolate fountain, breathing in the decadent scents of ripe berries and dark cocoa. Or at least, she had been until the waitress appeared with her champagne offering while the country band rocked on.

"No, thank you." Jessamyn held up a hand to refuse the alcohol, knowing she should start considering more facets of her diet than just avoiding champagne now that she was expecting a child. Her to-do list seemed to expand by the minute ever since she'd learned about the pregnancy.

It still felt surreal—and exciting—to think she carried a new life inside her. Ryder's baby.

As she plucked a raspberry from the dessert buffet, Jessamyn's gaze sought her date again. He stood near the now-vacant podium where the Atlas Foundation's president had made a short speech about Ryder's contributions to environmental awareness. Ryder was in conversation with a younger couple dressed in matching tuxedos who, she'd learned earlier in the evening, were significant donors to the charity.

She popped the berry in her mouth just as Ryder's blue eyes met hers across the photo booth area set up in front of a digital backdrop of Wakefield Ranch.

How was it that even so far from him, she experienced the tug of heated male interest? Rolling the berry on her tongue, she felt the answering awareness for Ryder, her skin flushing as he broke away from the pair he'd been speaking with to head her way.

She bit into the fruit as he stalked closer, never taking his gaze from her.

How could she be so breathless at the thought of touching him when he'd made it clear that his proposal was for a marriage of convenience because of their baby? Shouldn't that have dulled this fiery response to him? All at once she recalled Fleur's idea that sexual chemistry was nature's flashing neon sign to point her toward someone who could be The One.

Sage advice or silly?

As Ryder reached her, his palm slid around her waist to the small of her back. He leaned down to whisper, "I'll admit I'm curious about what thoughts put that particular expression on your face as I walked over here."

Her heart thumped harder. "Just wondering when we'll have time to talk." She tried to swallow down the breathlessness to focus on what was important tonight. "I received a phone call from Susan Wilson. Apparently you encouraged her to phone me?"

Ryder tensed beside her, guiding her a few steps away from the music and chatter growing louder as the dancing wore on. "She told you about the rescue on Longs Peak?"

She leaned back to gauge his expression as he continued to lead her out of the tent and onto the expanse of lawn that led to his house. If she didn't know better, she would think he sounded wary. Guarded. But her father's ex-girlfriend had spoken warmly about the search and rescue team she credited for saving her life.

"She did." Jessamyn had listened in growing anger to the woman's story as Susan explained how Mateo Barclay had led her up a path he was unfamiliar with, expecting her to make a climb well above her skill level. "I knew you were a part of the rescue team that day, but until I spoke with her, I had no idea how difficult it must have been for the first responders."

As Ryder moved them farther away from the party tent strung with white lights, it became more difficult to see his face under the quarter moon. He gestured toward a wrought iron bench near a windmill built to look antique, but Jessamyn had learned this evening that it provided considerable power for the house's electrical systems.

"I can't take any credit for the rescue," he clarified, shaking his head as he claimed a seat beside her, his knee brushing hers where the long slit of her dress bared one leg. "I was still learning and didn't play a prominent role."

She studied him in the moonlight as he tucked a finger into his bow tie, loosening it a fraction. The action prompted her to put a restraining hand on his.

"I didn't mean to steal you away before the party ended. Should we wait to speak further until we say good-night to your guests?"

She breathed in the pine scent of his aftershave while the minty aroma of bee balm drifted up from the flower beds nearby. She knew that it was more than just heightened senses from pregnancy that made her crave more of him.

His gaze swung to hers, his jaw flexing. "No. I've had this on my mind for a long time, Jessamyn. We need to talk now."

Wariness curled through her as she let go of him. Did he mean he wished to discuss the pregnancy instead? The idea didn't quite connect since he couldn't have had the baby on his mind for a long time. He'd only just found out she was expecting his child days ago.

Plus, his tone didn't bode well for the romantic possibilities of a future with Ryder that Fleur's encouraging words had led Jessamyn to start thinking about. Had she been foolish to begin hoping that he could have deeper feelings for her one day?

"All right, then, we can talk." She crossed her legs to make herself more comfortable on the cool metal seat. Fearing any real comfort wasn't in the cards for her this evening. "You know about Susan Wilson's call since you urged her to contact me. And while her take on my father affirms he's not the person I believed him to be, his behavior on the mountain that day won't help me win the court case."

In the brief silence after she spoke, the country band switched to something more down tempo, quieting the distant crowd underneath the glowing white pavilion. Jessamyn could see couples pairing off on the dance floor, heads inclining toward one another. She wished she was there with Ryder, still enjoying the feel of his hands on her instead of wading through whatever he had to say to her. Everything about his stiff shoulders and serious tone told her she wasn't going to like it.

"But I know something that will help you win the case, Jess." His voice was pitched low. He shifted on the bench to look her squarely in the eye, and she could see him better now that her vision had adjusted to the grayed-out shades of moonlight. "I learned something from your father while we waited for the rest of the search and rescue team to pull Susan up from the ledge where she'd fallen."

"*You* know something," Jessamyn repeated, regrouping mentally. "So you didn't bring me out here to talk about the baby?"

"I need to tell you this first." He swiped a hand through his dark hair, a horseshoe cuff link catching the party lights as he mussed sleek strands. "I hoped Susan might have been privy to the same information I learned that day, since she wouldn't have been under the confidentiality restrictions that have held me back."

Frowning, she tried to follow what he was saying. "I don't understand. What restrictions?"

He looped one arm over the back of the bench. "As a first responder, I operate under doctor-patient confidentiality expectations. It's more of a gray area for EMS workers, but courts have ruled that patients have a right to privacy during emergency care."

Her mind jumped ahead now, making new connections. "You learned something on the mountain that day? While treating my father? And her?"

As she swiveled in her seat toward him, her sequins caught awkwardly in the wrought iron, but that was the least of her concerns. What did Ryder know that could help her case?

"I had the least experience of the search and rescue crew, so I was tasked with keeping your father stable while we waited for the others to bring up Susan." He hadn't answered the questions, clearly having his own plan for sharing what he knew with her. Ryder's gaze slid from hers to look off into the distance, as if seeing other mountains in his mind. "Your dad was exhibiting symptoms of shock and distress."

"According to Susan, he hadn't checked her equipment before they started rappelling. And he had taken them on the wrong trail, so they were coming down a much tougher route than they'd climbed up." Jessamyn had learned this from the phone call. Also, that her father had been the one to end the relationship in the hospital, not the other way around. Susan had sustained multiple breaks in her legs and back and hadn't been able to return home for weeks. "I know that much."

Jessamyn owed her sisters and her mother an apology for ever taking their dad's side in the split. He'd kept a very dark side hidden from her. The call from Mateo's ex-girlfriend had underscored that, strengthening Jessamyn's resolve to distance herself from him.

Professionally, that might take time. But she refused to associate with someone who continually put selfish interests above hers.

Ryder shook his head slowly. "That's not the half of it."

"Tell me." Tension drew her whole body tight. Her relationship with her father had taken one hit after another ever since he'd filed the paperwork to contest the will.

Now it felt like she'd never known him at all.

"Mateo was wound up. Talking fast." Ryder's tone softened as his attention returned to her. He laid a hand on her arm, the warmth of his skin failing to ward off the chill of premonition that she wouldn't like what was coming. "He was expressing frustration with Susan, saying he preferred—his words—'strong women who could keep up.'"

Her throat hurt, sensing that this was going to get worse before it got better. "That doesn't surprise me, ugly though it may be. Go on."

How many times had her father expressed approval for her when she came into work sick or stayed in the office for long hours on the weekend to force through a deal? His brand of "win at all costs" wasn't healthy, but for years it had forced her to achieve more. She'd bought into the whole "live to work" idea hook, line and sinker, never making herself a priority.

Ryder scrubbed a hand over his face before continuing quietly. "Mateo confessed that's why he left your mom once she began to struggle with depression. He didn't have the time or patience for her illness."

A small sound escaped her throat. An echo of the despair her mother must have felt at being abandoned by the man who was supposed to care for her most in the world. God, Jessamyn had been so wrong to listen to his glib bs. And she'd been even more wrong to follow in his footsteps, putting work and a bottom line before family.

That hurt. But there was also another hurt underneath that. Another layer of raw ache as she met Ryder's eyes.

"All this time you knew how awful he was," she mused aloud, pulling away from his touch. How many bad decisions could she have avoided if she'd had this knowledge nine years ago. "And you allowed me to go on believing—"

"Wait." He cut her off, his voice sounding—impossibly—more tortured than her own. "Please. There's more."

She couldn't catch her breath, her whole world effectively rearranged by this conversation already. And there was more? She wrapped her arms around her midsection, as if she could protect the life inside her from this night of awful revelations.

The band in the pavilion was saying their goodnights to the remaining guests before recorded music switched on over the outdoor speaker system, an old-time country-western ballad. Guests were leaving the party, laughter and talk spilling out onto the pavement near the valet stand.

Beside her in the shadows, Ryder continued.

"Finally, Mateo told me that he knew his own mother disinherited him for being a jackass to his wife."

Everything inside her went still.

"He said those words?" She rounded on him, relief and anger knotting her insides. Ryder had just offered her the key to winning the will contest case. Too bad he'd withheld it from her for weeks while she turned Crooked Elm upside down for evidence he'd had all along. "Dad knew even then that Gran wasn't going to leave Crooked Elm to him?"

"That was my understanding. Yes."

"And you didn't tell me because of my father's

right to confidentiality?" Her voice went higher, disbelief creeping in.

She wasn't well versed in the law. But Ryder understood how much she'd followed in her father's footsteps. Knew how much doing so had cost her relationships with the rest of her family. And he'd chosen not to tell her a word of this when any one piece of it would have changed so many decisions she'd made since then. There had to be dozens of ways he could have steered her to the information about her father without outright telling her.

"Yes. A court could still refuse to admit a confession made during a time of duress—"

"Screw the court, Ryder." The angry words shot out before she could temper them. "What about *me*? Did I mean nothing to you once I left Catamount? Were you so hell-bent on breaking my heart ten years ago that you decided I didn't deserve to know this? That my father admitted all those awful things to you firsthand?"

Her sisters had always believed as much of their father, of course. But that was different than hearing her dad admit it all in his own words.

Thinking back to the timeline of when Ryder would have been on that mountain with her dad, Jessamyn realized they would have been broken up for a year at the time. Probably less. She'd gone to college in New York City specifically to live closer to her dad and to start interning at Barclay Property Group.

"I didn't even know if *now* was the right time,

Jess." Ryder spread his arms wide, a gesture of surrender. As if he was throwing himself at her mercy
now that she couldn't feel any. "Even if the letter of
the law is gray, the spirit of the law says I shouldn't
be telling you."

Cold hurt split her in half. How could she have
thought that he might grow to care for her just because they shared a physical connection? How many
times did Ryder have to prove that he would never
put her first before she got it through her head?

"Yet you decided to break nine years of silence
now, just when you find out I'm carrying your child?"

He started to speak, but she held up a hand, not
finished. Anger building.

"Could your sudden attack of scruples have anything to do with the fact that our child will be a future beneficiary of Crooked Elm if I win my case
against Dad?" Unable to sit beside him another moment, she stood quickly.

Started walking.

She needed to go home. Now.

"Jessamyn. Wait." Ryder's steps vibrated the
ground behind her. "It's you that I'm thinking of,
you, first and foremost. You that I want to protect—"

"By making me spin in circles for weeks trying
to find evidence that you've had all along?" She kept
coming back to that. "My father was not a patient.
He was the man responsible for injuring his girlfriend. And it's not like he confessed to something
that could come up in court. So I fail to see the big

ethical dilemma here. You didn't owe him anything, as far as I'm concerned. But me?"

She felt the burning behind her eyes. Knew she needed to get away from him before he saw how much he'd hurt her.

Deeply. Irreparably.

Gathering the last of her strength, she continued, "You did owe me something, Ryder. And you simply didn't care enough to make me a priority. Then. Now. Or ever."

What had he done?

Ryder banged his fist on the steering wheel of his truck half an hour later, pushing the accelerator too fast as he drove away from the party.

Thick darkness enfolded him as he rounded a bend above Wakefield Ranch, the truck whipping past trees as he wound toward the mountains. Climbing higher above Catamount.

He wanted to go to Jessamyn. Needed to talk to her. Explain himself in a way that would somehow make her understand—

But he couldn't go to Crooked Elm like this. Half out of his mind with fear that she would push him from her life for good. What about the child she carried?

He'd figured a drive would clear his head first, so he'd walked away from his duties as one of the Atlas Gala hosts and left his departing guests to the care of the foundation organizers. Jessamyn needed to be his priority, damn it. But he couldn't go to her until he sorted out his thoughts. Until he found the right words that would make her see that he'd done his best—

Another bend in the road came up too quickly. His headlights flashed onto tree trunks instead of twin yellow lines.

Braking too late, Ryder yanked the steering wheel hard to the left. Tires squealed. The truck cab tilted.

The whole vehicle lurched toward the trees and the mountain precipice beyond—

Before the truck stopped. Inches from the trunk of a gnarled old pine tree.

Ryder clutched the steering wheel in both hands, engine running but his anger gone. What the hell was he doing? He could have gone over that cliffside in a moment of anger and stupidity. He'd been moments away from needing a search and rescue team himself.

Like so many people he'd saved on the mountain over the last nine years, he'd taken his focus away from what was important.

Banging his fist on the steering wheel again— more gently this time—he knew he couldn't go to Jessamyn's tonight. He had no idea how to rescue this relationship, but he wouldn't find the answers in the dark tonight.

He would never forgive himself if he lost her. So he'd simply do whatever it took to win her back.

Thirteen

Eyes still burning from bitter tears even two days later, Jessamyn ignored the knocking on her bedroom door. Sliding a pillow over her head, she burrowed deeper in her covers, oblivious to the time of day.

She'd hardly left her bed at Crooked Elm since she'd returned home after the gala, barely speaking to Fleur since she couldn't talk without crying. Instead, she'd sent her sister texts from the privacy of her own room relating the gist of what had happened with Ryder. After half a lifetime of being one of those "strong women" her stupid father admired, she'd caved in on herself and could hardly draw a breath without falling apart. For herself. For the relationships she'd torched with her mom and sisters because of a man who hadn't deserved her faith. For the loss of what might have been with Ryder if he hadn't kept secrets from her. And, contrarily, she cried for the loss of Ryder's arms around her, too.

Ryder.

Just thinking about him made the tears threaten again. Wasn't there a limit to how much water could express through those tiny ducts in her eyes?

The circle of her futile thoughts was broken by more knocking at her door. Louder this time. *Rat. Tat. Tat.*

"Jess? It's Lark." Her sister's voice drifted through more softly. "Can I come in?"

Lark was here?

Jessamyn slid the pillow from over her head, sitting up in bed. A faded T-shirt from a long-ago summer camp fell in wrinkles. Her head pounded. Even her body ached from the monsoon of emotions brought on by Ryder's revelation.

"Lark?" Her voice scratched as she spoke for the first time in two days.

"I'm coming in," her older sister announced as she turned the handle, her voice as no-nonsense and authoritative as Jessamyn remembered from childhood. Lark had long taken her role as oldest Barclay sister seriously. "We need to talk."

Yes, they did. Jessamyn owed both of her sisters—and her mother—long and thorough apologies for not listening all the times they'd tried to tell her their father wasn't a good person.

And for so much more. She'd abandoned them

on Christmases and birthdays. She hadn't attended Lark's wedding or been there two years afterward when her older sister had gone through a divorce. Jessamyn *had* tried to send Fleur financial help for college over the years, but that was as much effort as she'd made, and Fleur had always sent back those checks.

Money was a poor excuse for connection. Real connection.

Now, as the bedroom door opened, Lark stepped onto the old blue-and-yellow braid rug, with Fleur on her heels. Lark wore a black knit sleeveless dress and matching sandals, her straight dark hair in a braid that lay on one shoulder. No jewelry. No makeup. Her bright green eyes were all the more noticeable for the lack of decoration, and a hundred old memories swept over Jessamyn. Lark bandaging skinned knees and kissing them better. Lark at the stove, just two years older than Jessamyn but light-years wiser, stirring the butter into their macaroni and cheese lunches. Lark dressed as a wicked witch for Halloween while Fleur and Jessamyn flitted around as good fairies.

She owed her big sister so much better than she'd given back. A wave of love flooded through her as Lark sank onto the foot of the bed without fanfare.

"How are you feeling?" Lark asked, green eyes running over her but taking in what must be an extraordinarily disheveled appearance without comment.

"Hungry, actually." Her hand went to her belly

as she recalled her biggest responsibility. "I should probably get something—"

"I'm on it," Fleur volunteered, still on her feet near the door. "You may recall I've tried to tempt you to eat about five different times, so I've got some really good things ready."

Their younger sister darted out through the open door, her copper-colored ponytail swishing as her bare feet moved soundlessly into the corridor.

Lark cleared her throat quietly. "Congratulations on the pregnancy." At Jessamyn's questioning look, Lark hastened to add, "Fleur filled me in on everything. And although you're obviously distressed today, I'm hoping you're feeling okay about the baby?"

More love bubbled up inside her. Not just for Lark being here with her, but for the child she carried.

"The pregnancy is definitely a good thing." Grabbing a downy pillow, she dragged it over her belly and hugged it to her, a small comfort for both her baby and her, too.

Lark's steady gaze was as calming as her voice when she pressed, "But Fleur said you haven't come out of your room for two days."

It was easy to envision her sister in her role as a therapist, helping people to navigate problems and relationships.

"I've been reeling since Ryder's disclosure at the Atlas Gala," she confessed, swiping a hank of unwashed hair from her face. "While I wish I could say it's been pregnancy hormones that have turned my emotions into a waterfall for days, it has more to do with learning the truth about Dad. And learning it from the father of my child, who's known what a sorry excuse for a human being our father has been this whole time."

Nodding slowly, Lark seemed to take this in. She didn't comment at first. Getting to her feet, she walked to an open window and rolled up the shade where sheer curtains filtered the pinks and yellows of a setting sun.

"Why do you think you found it tougher to hear the truth about Dad from Ryder?" Lark asked as she adjusted the curtains, carefully spacing them on the rods, so they billowed evenly in an evening breeze.

Jessamyn blinked at the unexpected question. She was grateful that Fleur reentered the room with a tray, buying Jessamyn time to think about her answer while the scents of yeasty bread and warm ginger swirled under her nose.

Fleur settled the red metal tray on the nightstand. "I have more nutritious things downstairs, but I wasn't sure if you were having morning sickness so I didn't want to overwhelm you with anything that might trigger your stomach."

"Thank you so much." Jessamyn reached for the warm French bread and took a bite.

"That's ginger tea, by the way. It's supposed to be good in early pregnancy." Fleur folded her legs beneath her as she settled on the bed in the spot Lark had vacated.

Fleur's turquoise bead bracelets and white eyelet

top reminded Jessamyn of the way their grandmother had always dressed, although Fleur paired hers with denim cutoffs instead of the long jean skirts Antonia had favored. Or maybe it was the freshly baked foods and perpetually warm kitchen that had Jessamyn thinking about Gran.

"So?" Lark's voice interrupted the run of nostalgia. "Is there a reason it bothered you so much more to hear about Dad from Ryder than it did from us? Or Mom? Or his ex-girlfriend?"

Jessamyn set aside the bread she'd been eating, recognizing that this wasn't Lark's counselor voice. This was her annoyed-sister voice. And with good reason.

"I am deeply, genuinely sorry I didn't listen all the times you tried to tell me about him. I think I saw what I needed him to be, and maybe it will take time for me to understand why." Perhaps she really had seen herself in him, and considering what she knew about him now, that was a gut punch.

Still, she thought—she hoped—she was a good person. Her father had broken up with his injured girlfriend in the hospital when he'd been to blame for the woman's fall. Jessamyn would never end a relationship when someone needed her—

A flicker of memory from the night of the gala returned. Ryder's voice sounded in her mind.

Nothing is more important to me than ensuring we're on the same page for our child's future. They never had gotten around to discussing the baby after the gala. Regret for her emotional departure niggled. As a mother, she needed to start putting her child first.

And about how she'd treated Ryder...?

"Mom and Dad's personal war did a number on us all, Jess," Lark assured her as she moved to the next window and repeated the procedure—shade up, curtains precisely adjusted. "Since moving to specialize in child therapy, I have all the more appreciation for the emotional hellfire we waded through as kids, so this isn't about blame. I'm genuinely wondering why you were able to finally recognize the truth when Ryder said it?"

Because she trusted him deeply. She'd recognized his innate goodness and caring at eighteen years old and she'd loved him even then. But she'd loved her sisters, too. Even when she didn't trust their view of their father.

"Maybe because he was outside the family." Tentatively, she picked up the mug of steaming tea and took a sip, hoping to warm the chill from her heart. "He didn't tell me to try to make me abandon Dad. Ryder shared it because the court case is coming up, and he knew that Antonia wanted the land to go to us."

The tea was delicious, and she drank a little more.

"Ryder has no horse in the race. He's just a good person trying to do the right thing." Lark repeated it simply. As if it were a statement of fact. "If anything, his keeping the secret that long speaks to his character...the kind of character anyone would want in a man."

Jessamyn bristled. She jostled the mug a little and had to set down the tea.

"Keeping me in the dark while I made bad decision after bad decision was the right thing to do?" The frustration stirred again. "He could have told me—hinted to me—nine years ago, but—"

"But he tried to keep an oath he swears in his profession. The confidentiality clause isn't there as a suggestion or a guideline. It's a law." Lark's green, older-sister eyes bored into hers with the same wisdom she'd always possessed. "And knowing the kind of man Mateo Barclay is, Ryder could face a lawsuit from Dad if he makes those words public for our sake."

The idea made her ill.

"God." She retrieved the mug again, craving the tea to soothe the sudden nausea that was more about Ryder's predicament than any morning sickness. "Dad is lawsuit-happy."

"So maybe you shouldn't be too hard on Ryder," Fleur suggested, laying a hand on Jessamyn's ankle through the blankets. "If he comes forward, we definitely have a stronger shot of defending Gran's will. But it could come at a cost to Ryder."

Fleur's eyes were as kind as her gentle words.

"Maybe I lashed out where I shouldn't have." More qualities she shared with her dad? Steeling herself to do better, Jessamyn forced herself to dig deeper. To share the feelings under the anger. "I was just so hurt that he kept it from me when I wanted—for once—to feel important to him."

Ryder was a good man. She'd known it a decade ago, and he'd apparently been wrestling with ethical issues she hadn't fully appreciated. Perhaps instead of seeking a declaration from him—hoping he'd declare feelings for her that he just didn't have for her yet—maybe she should be more focused on being worthy of him.

She'd been toying with the idea of staying in Catamount. Living closer to Ryder so he could be a part of their child's life. Besides, she'd dreamed of coming back here one day, before her life became one endless list of achievements to accomplish.

There were opportunities for creative real estate development here. Ways Jessamyn could make her mark on this part of Colorado.

"You are important to him," Fleur promised. "He called the house phone earlier when you didn't reply to his messages. He sounded worried about you."

Or worried about the baby.

Which was his right, as the child's father, even if it hurt that his concern was more for the pregnancy.

Whatever happened between them, Jessamyn couldn't simply ignore him because she was hurt that he didn't love her back. She owed him more than that.

"I'll call him." Setting aside the tea, she slid out from the covers, knowing she needed to make things right with a lot of people. "But first, I want you both to know that I'm going to put in hard work to fix my relationships with you and with Mom. And if there's one thing I'm good at, it's hard work."

Lark folded her arms, assessing her. "In that case, I'll look forward to being impressed."

Fleur made a dismissive sound as she rose to hug Jessamyn. "I'm already on board, Jess. I wanted us all at Crooked Elm this summer so we could patch up our differences and be a family again."

Jessamyn's throat closed up at her sister's easy forgiveness. A few more tears came, but this time, she didn't mind. If only one person was ready to forgive her, that was progress.

She squeezed her sibling tightly. "I never stopped loving you, even when I wasn't in your life. I hope you know that." Cracking open one eye, she glanced at Lark over Fleur's shoulder. "That goes for you, too."

"Excellent." Lark gave a satisfied nod but didn't move closer. "I'm facing the worst summer of my life now that Gibson is returning to Catamount while I'm here. So you can start showing the love by lying to him every single day he asks about me and telling him I'm *not* here."

Jessamyn let go of Fleur, her mind filling up with questions. Star hockey player Gibson Vaughn was in Catamount? She knew that was big news. There'd been rumors he would take a contract as a free agent, but maybe he was retiring at last. But even as she wanted to quiz her, their truce was so new—fragile—she accepted this wasn't the time to push Lark.

Before she even finished the thought, Fleur caught her eye and gave a discreet shake of her head as if to keep her quiet. A moot point since Lark walked out of the bedroom, back straight and chin high.

Jessamyn didn't envy her sister having to face her famous ex-husband. The sports media hadn't been kind to her during her brief marriage to Gibson.

"I'll fill you in another time," Fleur whispered as she picked up the abandoned food tray. "You should go see a man about a baby."

The reality of what Jessamyn needed to do returned, weighing down her feet.

She knew she needed to see Ryder. To smooth things over for her outsize reaction to an admission that hadn't been easy for him. No matter how much it hurt to face a man who didn't love her—who'd only proposed because he was the most kind and honorable of men—she still had to own up to make things right between them.

She would preserve a friendship between them. Open communication and goodwill for the sake of their child. Not for anything would she repeat her parents' mistakes. Somehow, she would pull herself together to visit Ryder.

They had their baby's future to plan.

Standing inside a quiet paddock as night fell, Ryder waited impatiently for a veterinarian to arrive to help him with a mare ready to foal. He stroked the nose of the agitated dun while a warm night breeze blew through her dark mane.

At least Coco's foaling would give him something to occupy his thoughts tonight. Maybe the birthing would buy him a few hours that weren't filled with regrets about how he'd handled things with Jessamyn. Had there been a minute so far that he hadn't thought about her walking away from him after the Atlas Gala? The ache in his chest hadn't eased for even a second since he'd watched her fight back tears because of him. He'd gone to sleep both nights since the evening of the gala knowing he'd put that hurt in her eyes and hating himself for it.

Coco snorted and pawed at the grass, reminding him to keep his focus. Where was the vet? He'd thought the doctor had arrived a few minutes ago when he spotted headlights by the main house, but there was no sign of the woman yet.

In the meantime, Ryder had turned the animal out into the clean grass for foaling since the mustang had a history of difficult births and she liked her space to roll around at the end. He hoped the paddock would be the right choice for her.

At least he knew something about mares and he could offer some help. Unlike with Jessamyn, who didn't want to see him or talk to him after he'd withheld what he knew about her father.

The horse paced away from him to kick at her belly, her unrest driving his own.

Checking his phone, he tracked the vet on the app for the animal practice and saw the woman was still half an hour away. So who had been pulling up to the main house a little while ago?

"Ryder?" A familiar woman's voice called from the far side of the barn.

Jessamyn.

Was he dreaming that he heard her voice now? Or was it possible she was really here?

"Back here," he called through the dark, wishing he'd switched on the outdoor lights over the paddock. He'd flipped them off earlier in Coco's labor, hoping it might relax her.

"It's hard to see," Jessamyn remarked, her voice registering surprise but no anger. No coolness.

"Sorry about that. I switched the lights off in the hope of settling an anxious mare ready to foal tonight." He knew better than to hope she'd forgiven him for staying silent about her dad. But if there was any chance she would hear him out again about a future together, he intended to remind her why they should be in each other's lives.

And he'd do a better job of it than he had on Sawmill Mountain when he'd first learned about the baby. He'd processed the news. Understood there was nothing more important to him in the world than being there for his child.

Except being there for Jessamyn. Whatever it took.

"It's fine. I've got my phone's flashlight."

Ryder turned on his phone again and raised it over his head to help her see. "I'm by the paddock."

He spotted her shadow moving closer and the blue light of her cell phone as well. She shone the flashlight feature at the ground, illuminating her legs in dark jeans and boots. A far cry from the way she'd been dressed the last time he'd seen her. Yet, as she came fully into focus by the light of his phone, every bit as beautiful and more.

His heart gave a rough thump at her nearness. But these days, it beat for her.

"Is this a bad time?" she asked, her voice betraying trepidation.

Nerves?

He didn't think that could be the case. Still, he reached a hand automatically to steady her step. Or maybe just because he was dying to touch her, however briefly.

She wore a pale-colored T-shirt, so her arm was bare where he touched her. The skin so smooth and soft it took all his restraint not to pull her closer.

"Not at all," he reassured her, ignoring his impulses to guide her toward the paddock rail so she could orient herself. "Just watching over Coco until the vet gets here. The mare has had trouble foaling in the past, so I don't want to leave her."

"Do you think she'll mind that I'm here?" she asked, turning off her phone and slipping the device into the back pocket of her jeans. "I don't want to upset her."

"Maybe she'll appreciate a woman's presence," he mused, settling against the paddock rail beside her. It felt right to stand next to her, to share his daily concerns with her.

"I only know a little more about horses than I do about giving birth, so I'm not sure how helpful I'll be." Jessamyn folded her arms over the top rail, leaning into the fence. "I didn't pay much attention to farm life back then."

He could see her clearly now in the moonlight, her delicate features calling to his fingers to trace them. Part of him was dying to know why she was here and if she felt even a fraction of the regret he did about their parting the other night.

But the other part of him feared she was coming to tell him goodbye.

"You know plenty about horses." He wished he'd taken more time to reminisce with her while he'd had the chance. To bring to mind the fun things they'd done together that summer when they'd fallen for each other, back when Jessamyn had still worn her heart on her sleeve. "I used to love watching you barrel race in the junior competitions."

Coco still paced the paddock, but she seemed less agitated now. Was she comforted by their low voices?

Jessamyn turned to him, her brows raised. A half smile kicked up the corner of her lips. "You never told me that."

"You were just a kid then," he reminded her. "So it was hardly the kind of thing I'd say to woo you when you were eighteen and I was an oh-so-smooth nineteen. But yeah, I remember you barrel racing. You did it like you tackle everything—focused, determined. Hell-bent."

He was enjoying the memory so much he didn't realize she'd turned away from him again until her voice sounded sadly. "Ha. Sounds like me. All about the accomplishment. Never about the people."

Surprised, he laid a hand on her arm again, hungry to correct the impression.

"Are you kidding me? That couldn't be further from the truth." Another old memory stirred. "Do you remember the year you won the juniors?"

He could feel her pulse thrum at her wrist and couldn't resist the urge to stroke his thumb lightly over the spot.

"The day my parents got into a screaming match in the stands, and Fleur launched into a rendition of 'America the Beautiful' to try to take the arena's focus away from the brawl breaking out?" Jessamyn shook her head, her loose hair glinting in the moonlight. "Unfortunately, yes."

Squeezing her arm gently, he leaned closer to make his point.

"When the whole arena was gossiping about Fleur's performance, whispering about the precocious nine-year-old in spangles for somehow hogging the spotlight, I saw you give her the trophy you won to cheer her up." It had been a sweet moment. A brief glimpse he'd caught of a dejected nine-year-old being comforted by her big sister.

He'd been fourteen at the time, sitting in the mostly empty arena eating as much fried dough as his bottomless stomach could hold. And he'd never forgotten that small moment of kindness.

"I'd forgotten that," she admitted, straightening as Coco paced toward them, head down. "I can't believe you noticed us that day."

Jessamyn held her free hand out to the mare, letting Coco's restless nose move over her palm. Jess hadn't moved her other arm away from him where his fingers still circled her wrist. Thumb still hovering over the pulse point.

"I've always noticed you. And you're good with people." He needed her to know that. No matter if she was here to tell him goodbye, he had to make sure she understood what he saw in her. "I don't need to live in New York to know that's why you excel at your job there. People put their trust in you because you earn it, and that's a very attractive quality."

Her eyes remained on Coco as the mare whinnied softly. Jessamyn comforted her with a stroke down her neck.

The moment was broken by the momentary splash of white headlights across their faces. The sound of crunching gravel on the far side of the barn.

"That must be the vet." Letting go of Jess's arm, he moved toward the barn. "I'd better turn on the lights so she can see her way back here."

Ten minutes later, he had the lights on and the doctor set up in the paddock to check Coco. The vet had brought a student intern with her to help with the birth, so Ryder hadn't bothered calling in anyone else to sit with them.

Giving him the time he craved with Jessamyn.

"Would you like to sit on the porch swing?" he suggested, gesturing toward the back of the main house where a wide veranda wrapped the whole length. "I can get us drinks, or—"

He trailed off since she was shaking her head.

"I'm fine. But if you think it's okay to leave Coco, the porch swing sounds good."

Ryder glanced back toward the paddock, now well lit by the exterior barn lights. "Coco is in good hands. She looks more comfortable this time. I think she'll like being outdoors instead of the birthing stall."

They walked side by side in silence for a few moments, stars winking overhead, night bugs humming. Tension ratcheted higher inside him as he braced himself for whatever she'd come here to say.

He glanced over at her to see her frowning. Biting her lip.

Was she wondering how to say she was leaving?

By the time they reached the porch swing, he couldn't hold back his own words any longer.

Steadying the chain swings so she could make herself comfortable, he blurted, "Jess, I'm so sorry I didn't tell you about your father sooner. You were right—"

"No." She ignored the swing seat to clutch his shoulder where he stood. "No, I *wasn't* right. You were, Ryder. I came here to apologize to *you* for making it all about me when you were torn between ethical responsibility and wanting to help me."

His grip on the chain tightened. He couldn't quite believe what she'd just said, which seemed like a total about-face from the other night.

"But what you said about your father not being the patient, that was true. I don't think he was ever technically admitted to the hospital." Ryder had revisited the encounter so many times in his mind, trying to untwine what he owed to Mateo Barclay versus what he owed to Jessamyn.

Every time, he wished he'd spoken to Jessamyn sooner. Because right or wrong, he was glad she knew now.

"He was in shock." Jessamyn's fingers dug lightly into his shoulder as if she could press the idea into him. "Lark thought Dad could even sue you if you made a statement about—"

"Let him." He waved it off, unconcerned with whatever civil nonsense Mateo cooked up with an expensive attorney. The only thing he cared about right now was having Jessamyn here, her hands on him. Her hazel eyes full of concern for him. "I will go on record in court about what I heard that day, and I hope like hell it helps you and your sisters win your case because I know what Antonia wanted for Crooked Elm. I've done my best to uphold the oath of providing emergency care, but if I lose my certification over this, it's still a choice I will stand by because you're my priority, Jessamyn. You and our baby."

Crickets chirped and branches rustled overhead to fill the silence as the words seemed to settle around her.

Was it his imagination, or did her expression soften somehow? Her hold on him eased, her hand sliding down his arm with slow care.

"Ryder." A wealth of emotion hid behind the single word.

He was certain of it.

Because she was leaving Catamount and him for good?

Or because she might give him another chance?

Before he could find out, she continued, "One way or another, my sisters and I will defend Gran's will. Call it pregnancy intuition, but I feel it in my bones that we're going to prevail." A small smile lifted one side of her mouth. "My sisters and I are coming together in a way I would have never predicted. And it just feels—right. Like together, we're going to win this thing and prove to Dad that he can't call the shots forever."

She sounded certain. Confident.

And he was glad for her. But she hadn't said anything about staying in Catamount. With him.

"Jessamyn. I'll do everything I can to help. I promise you." His hands went to her waist in his need for her to listen. To make her see they weren't finished here yet. "But it's also important to me that you know we belong together. We always have. Please don't leave Catamount without giving this—giving us—one more chance to be a family."

"I want that, too, Ryder. So much." Her eyes turned brighter, the tears pooling without falling.

"So what's holding you back?" He stroked her dark hair, hating that he'd brought her a moment's unhappiness. Not knowing what he was missing. "I'd give you my name. My whole world. I'd give up the ranch for part of the year to be in New York with you if that's what it takes—"

"I'd never ask that of you." A tear spilled down her

cheek, and he captured it with his thumb, wishing he could stop the flow forever. "You belong here."

You do, too. But he wouldn't be the one to tell her that if she didn't see it yet.

"Then let's get married and make this work," he urged, his hand cupping her face. "And know that I'm willing to do whatever it takes."

He could swear they were on the verge of understanding one another. Of being the family that he knew they were meant to be.

Her fingers fisted in the front of his T-shirt.

"I love you, Ryder," she admitted with a fierceness he'd never heard in her voice before. "And as much as I want that future with you, I won't marry you until you return some of the love I have for you. That I've had for you since I was eighteen years old."

Her fingers twisted the fabric tighter and he wondered how she could not know that she had his whole heart right in her hand? How could he have missed saying those words, especially since he knew the scars left by her parents' loveless marriage?

She needed—deserved—the reassurance.

"Oh, Jess." His forehead fell to hers, the relief of her words damn near taking his knees out from under him even as he grieved his blindness in missing what she needed from him. "How can you not know how much I love you, too?"

She edged back to study him, hazel eyes wide. Confused. Wary.

He cursed himself to hell and back.

Then, cradling her beautiful face in his hands, he

looked into the eyes that held his world and repeated the words that gave shape to everything he'd ever felt for this woman.

"I love you, Jessamyn Barclay. Forever and for always." His thumb stroked her cheek. He kissed one eyelid and then the other. "And that love is going to burn bright for you until I have you in my arms every day and in my bed every night."

He felt her shiver against him and pulled her tighter.

"You won't have long to wait," she promised, tilting her head to slant her lips over his. She kissed him with slow deliberation, tongue twining around his and turning him inside out before she edged back again. "Because I want that as soon as possible, do you hear me?"

He wasn't losing her. She was here to move into his life and she was never leaving it again.

Joy speared his insides.

"I hear you." He tugged her lower lip into his mouth, needing to taste more of her. "And I want to work out all the logistics of this new life of ours with you in the morning over breakfast, because we have a lot of figuring out to do for us and for our baby, too."

"Good. I've already figured out that I want to start my own development group out here so I can make Catamount my home. I'll still maintain a share of Barclay Property Group since I won't allow my father to shut me out of a company I helped him build. But there's nothing stopping me from starting another business of my own here." She wound slender arms around his neck, her breasts pressing against his chest. "But together, you and I can fine-tune all the necessary plans to be together."

They would face the future—whatever it held—side by side.

He shook his head, mesmerized by this fearless, ambitious woman. "I'd love that. But first, I'm taking you upstairs—"

"Less talking, cowboy," she purred against his lips as she tilted her hips into him. "More taking."

Counting his blessings, he swept Jessamyn Barclay right off her feet and did exactly as the lady asked.

* * * * *

Don't miss a single
Return to Catamount novel
by USA TODAY *bestselling author*
Joanne Rock!

Rocky Mountain Rivals
One Colorado Night
A Colorado Claim

Available exclusively from
Harlequin Desire.

SPECIAL EXCERPT FROM

(H) HARLEQUIN

DESIRE

*Finding his father's assistant at an underground fight
club, playboy Mason Kane realizes he isn't the only one
leading a double life. So he offers Charlotte Westbrook
a whirlwind Riviera fling to help her loosen up, but it
could cost her job and her heart...*

Read on for a sneak peek at
Secret Lives After Hours
by Cynthia St. Aubin

They stood facing each other, the summer heat still
radiating up from the sidewalk, the sultry breath of a
coming storm sifting through their hair.

Now.

Now was the moment where she would pull out her
phone, bring up the ride app. Bid him good-night. If she
did this, the past three hours could be bundled into a box
neither of them would ever have to open again. He might
smile at her secretly every now and then, wink at her
in acknowledgment, but that would be the end of it.

If she left now.

"Come up," Mason said.

It wasn't a question. It wasn't even an invitation.

It was an answer.

An answer to her own admission in the elevator. That she liked looking at him. That she could look at him more if she wanted.

That he wanted her to.

"Okay," Charlotte said.

Don't miss what happens next in...
Secret Lives After Hours *by Cynthia St. Aubin,*
the next book in The Kane Heirs series!
Available August 2022 wherever
Harlequin Desire books and ebooks are sold.

Harlequin.com

Love Harlequin romance?

DISCOVER.

Be the first to find out about promotions, news and exclusive content!

Facebook.com/HarlequinBooks

Twitter.com/HarlequinBooks

Instagram.com/HarlequinBooks

Pinterest.com/HarlequinBooks

YouTube.com/HarlequinBooks

ReaderService.com

EXPLORE.

Sign up for the Harlequin e-newsletter and download a free book from any series at **TryHarlequin.com**

CONNECT.

Join our Harlequin community to share your thoughts and connect with other romance readers!
Facebook.com/groups/HarlequinConnection

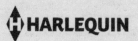